KILLER TRAIL

Whisper Island Mysteries - 1

Jenny Elaine

BOOKS BY JENNY ELAINE

ROSE OF SAVANNAH SERIES

The Healing Rose of Savannah
The Whispering Shadows of Savannah

SHADY PINES MYSTERY SERIES

Secrets from the Past
Lost in the Past
Storms of the Past
Shadows of the Past

WHISPER ISLAND MYSTERY SERIES

Killer Trail
Killer Pursuit

IN MEMORY OF SMUTTI, AN
ANGEL WRAPPED IN FUR.

PROLOGUE

The sun was beginning to set, and as its brilliant hues reflected off the coastal marshland, the brownish-green grass was suddenly turned into liquid gold. The Savannah River wound its way peacefully through the marsh, and ten-year-old Zaylie Layne stretched high onto her tip-toes as she tried to catch a glimpse of dolphins. A warm, salty breeze ruffled through her auburn hair, and the squawking of seagulls could be heard from above. Suddenly, a silvery-gray fin poked above the river's surface, and then another, only to disappear again just as quickly. Zaylie sucked in a breath and smiled widely, clapping her hands in excitement.

Whisper Island was thirty minutes from Savannah, Georgia. It had gotten its name from the Indians who'd inhabited the island first; they'd claimed the way the breeze from the ocean rustled through the trees and sea oats sounded like the whisper of their ancestors.

Zaylie loved this place and the roots she had here. Her father's family had owned Azalea Bluff, a small corner of the island, for nearly one hundred years. Now, as she looked out over the water, she could almost picture her great-grandfather out in the boat her father had told her about, casting his net into the river and pulling it back in, filled with shrimp.

"Zaylie, it's time to come in for your bath!"

Turning her head, Zaylie spotted her older sister, Zoe, waving to her from the back porch. Their parents had driven across the causeway to Savannah to celebrate their wedding anniversary, and Zoe had insisted she was old enough to babysit. Knowing she'd be in trouble later if she didn't mind her sister, Zaylie sighed and ran up the hill toward the house.

The giant old home looked glorious against the brilliantly colored evening sky. Zaylie called it "the mansion by the sea" and often pretended to be a mermaid or a pirate searching for buried treasure. Built in 1897, the white, two-story home stood proudly on a hill overlooking the Savannah River, its double chimneys and wraparound porch so full of history that she often wished the old place could talk. Her father was raised here, and her mother's family lived only a couple of miles away. It was a beautiful, peaceful place, and Zaylie loved living there.

"If you hurry, I'll draw with you after you're finished taking your bath," Zoe said as Zaylie climbed up the back porch steps.

Her eyes brightening, Zaylie nodded eagerly and hurried up the stairs. Zoe was fifteen and usually too busy with friends to play games with her little sister, so Zaylie was excited to get to spend the time together. She absolutely adored her sister. Zoe was smart and beautiful, and Zaylie had already decided she wanted to be just like her when she grew up.

After her bath, Zoe showed Zaylie how to draw a field of sunflowers. Zoe was a very talented artist, and Zaylie loved it when her sister would take the time to teach her how to create something from scratch. It was very rewarding to see all the hard work come together in the end, but Zaylie struggled with ever getting started in the first place. She could picture things in her mind, but capturing it on paper was often very difficult. Not for Zoe, though. Her beautiful hazel eyes would sparkle when she was inspired to draw, and during those moments of inspiration, her fingers would fly across the paper until the masterpiece was complete. She planned to go to Savannah College of Art and Design once she graduated from high school, and Zaylie just knew her sister would be famous someday.

They'd just finished with the sketching and were about to add color when an odd sound suddenly came from downstairs. Zaylie didn't pay much attention to it, but Zoe sat up straight and turned her head toward the bedroom door as she listened intently.

"I'll be right back," she muttered.

Zaylie nodded, her attention directed toward her drawing as Zoe stood and walked quietly from the room. A loud creak on the stairs echoed down the hall then, and Zaylie looked up in surprise when

Zoe came rushing back into the room. Her face was pale with fright as she quickly closed the door and locked it. Her eyes darted around the room as if searching for something.

"What's wrong, Zoe?" Zaylie asked.

"There's someone in the house," Zoe whispered, and the panic in her voice sent chills down Zaylie's spine.

Rushing across the room, Zoe grabbed her sister by the hand and dragged her toward the closet. Pushing Zaylie inside, she said, "I'm going to call the police. Stay in here and don't make a sound, okay? Promise?"

Zaylie nodded, her heart pounding as Zoe shut the closet door and wedged a chair against it.* There were small slats in the door, and Zaylie could see her sister's shadow as she hurried toward the cordless phone that sat by her bedside.

Just then, the bedroom door crashed open, and Zaylie heard her sister scream. Covering her mouth, Zaylie tried to see who the intruder was but couldn't make out anything other than light, figures, and shadows.

"What do you want?" Zoe asked in a trembling voice.

"I want a lot of things, babe, and you just happen to be one of them."

Zaylie strained to hear what the man was saying; his voice was low and menacing, and something about it sounded strange. She could see his dark figure as it crept slowly across the room toward

4

her sister.

"My parents will be home soon," Zoe told him, and Zaylie's heart caught at the fear in her voice. "Y-you won't get away with this."

The man chuckled. "I could get away with the moon if I wanted to."

Suddenly, he launched himself across the room, and Zoe screamed again. There was the sound of breaking glass, and Zaylie could hear the two struggling. Her heart pounding, Zaylie grabbed the doorknob and desperately tried to get out of the closet. When the door wouldn't open, she pounded on it with all her might, but it wouldn't budge. Pressing her face against the slats, she could see his dark figure as he dragged Zoe from the room, and sobs filled her throat. She took a step back and began to kick at the door with her bare feet, ignoring the pain that immediately shot through her toes and up her leg. She had to get out of there and help her sister. She *had* to.

She could hear Zoe's cries as the man forced her out into the hallway and down the stairs. Fear and panic grasped at Zaylie's heart as she continued to pound at the closet door, but it was no use. She was too small and weak to escape this prison of darkness, and when she heard the front door slam loudly downstairs, she stopped to listen. Her breathing was labored and her heart pounded, but the house was eerily quiet. With a loud sob, Zaylie fell to her knees and covered her face with her bruised hands. It was too late; she knew that. No one could help her sister now.

CHAPTER 1

T he bells jingled loudly in the distance, the sound steadily drawing closer and closer. Zaylie stopped and listened, her breathing heavy from all the running. She knew it was only a matter of time before they reached her.

It was mid-day, but the sun was covered by clouds, and the thick trees overhead made it hard to see. The jingling grew louder, and twigs and branches began to snap, causing a stir in the otherwise quiet forest. Zaylie squinted, her eyes searching until they found what they were looking for.

There she was; a black shadow slipping seamlessly through the bushes, her golden eyes stark and glaring against the darkness of the forest. Zaylie waited, standing completely still until she drew closer, her breathing also heavy. She stopped a couple of feet away and gave one sharp bark. Zaylie offered her some water, but she was much too focused to be distracted.

"Smutti, show me," Zaylie said, and the dog immediately turned to run in the direction from which she'd just come.

Zaylie took a quick sip from her water bottle and hurried after Smutti, her heart pounding. She was exhausted after the long trek but knew they couldn't quit now. They were getting close; she could feel it.

A young woman vanished without a trace the week before while on a camping trip in the mountains of West Virginia. She was vacationing there with her family when she decided to take a walk early one morning and never returned. The family searched for hours before calling the police for help. Local bloodhounds were brought to the scene and immediately picked up her trail, only to lose it the further they went. The police called off the search after only five days, and when Zaylie read about it in the newspaper, the father's desperate cry for help clutched at her heart. That's when she'd decided to offer her services.

Smutti, her black German Shepherd, was one of the best search and rescue dogs in America, and Zaylie was her handler. They'd flown in that morning and immediately set out to work. The girl's brother and a local volunteer led them to the place where the hounds lost the trail, and as Smutti got to work, Zaylie slowly walked around, her eyes carefully searching the ground.

"Do you think your dog can find what the hounds couldn't?" Kaleb, one of the volunteers, asked hopefully.

"If there's a scent to be found, she'll find it," Zaylie replied, squatting down to take a closer look at the ground in the area Smutti was smelling.

"But why did the hounds lose it?" Aaron, the

girl's brother, wanted to know.

"They track the ground only, so if there's a lot of cross-contamination or if the trail goes cold, they can no longer find any scent to follow," she explained. "Smutti, on the other hand, is special because she is cross-trained. She has the ability to follow a scent on the ground *and* in the air."

"I wouldn't think there would be much cross-contamination way out here, so why would the trail have gone cold?" Aaron asked, his brow knit in confusion.

"For this reason right here," Zaylie pointed to the ground, her chest tightening. Beneath some leaves was a smudged footprint, one that was much too large to belong to the missing girl. "It looks as if someone may have carried her away from here."

A soft breeze ruffled the auburn curls around her neck, and Zaylie watched as Smutti stopped sniffing the ground and immediately raised her head, her nose twitching. She'd caught a scent. With a sharp bark, she took off into the woods, leaving them to quickly follow the jingling of her collar. She never roamed too far, though. She would either stop and wait for Zaylie to catch up, or she'd come back for her handler. Just in case, though, Zaylie always attached a GPS collar to her neck.

Seconds passed, swiftly turning into minutes. The terrain was rough, and the air grew chilly the higher up they climbed. They placed little flags along the way, marking the trail as they went. Smutti led them to a place on the ground near a small creek that looked disturbed, and as Zaylie stooped down to investigate, she saw what appeared to be tiny little droplets of blood.

Suddenly, a yelp sounded from behind, and she swiftly turned to find Aaron slumped on the ground, clutching his ankle.

Kaleb and Zaylie quickly ran to his side. "What happened?" she asked, wincing at the look of pain on his face.

"I think…" he gasped, "I think it's broken."

"He tripped on that," Kaleb stated, nodding his head in the direction of an extruding tree root.

After a few moments of deliberation, it was decided that Kaleb would go back down the mountain for help while Zaylie stayed with Aaron.

After Kaleb had gone, Aaron begged her to continue searching. "I know you found something over there," he said, nodding towards the blood on the ground. "We're close, I know we are, and if we wait until Kaleb gets back, it'll be too dark to go on. Here," he said, reaching into his backpack to pull out a small handgun. "Take this and keep searching. Please."

Zaylie couldn't tell him no. His sister was out there, possibly badly hurt, and Zaylie felt just as he did; they were getting close. She wrapped a blanket around his shoulders, handed him the knife from her own backpack, and promised she'd be back soon.

Nearly twenty minutes had passed when Smutti

alerted Zaylie to a new find. She was tense and antsy, and Zaylie knew she'd found something solid this time. Feeling that she should be extra cautious, Zaylie took the bells from Smutti's collar and left them lying on the ground next to a marker.

"Show me," she said. As Smutti turned to run, Zaylie quickly added, "Walk," and the dog slowed down to trot by her master's side.

They walked through the forest, twigs and leaves snapping and crunching beneath their feet. There were, however, no other sounds to be heard. The birds were quiet, the squirrels still, and even the breeze seemed to have stopped. It gave Zaylie the uneasy feeling of being completely alone and isolated, while at the same time, chills ran up and down her spine as if they were being watched.

Smutti stopped then and Zaylie squinted, peering through the trees. There appeared to be a cabin just up ahead, and she quickly pulled the gun from her pocket. Slowly, dog and owner eased their way closer, their bodies moving as one. Just before stepping out into the clearing behind the cabin, Zaylie stopped, trying to decide what to do. She couldn't see through the windows, as they were covered by what appeared to be old rags, but there was a back door that she could go through. If it was unlocked.

Telling Smutti to "stay", Zaylie took a deep breath and began to move closer. She eased up the rickety steps, gun in hand, and slowly turned the doorknob. It rotated easily under her fingers, and she gently pushed the door open, her heart pounding.

The one-room cabin was dark with cobwebs hanging from the ceiling. She squinted, peering inside, her eyes taking in the old, dusty furniture, the unwashed plate on the kitchen table, and the cot that rested on the opposite side. Her eyes widened when she realized a still, unmoving form rested beneath the cot's covers.

She rushed across the room, and with trembling fingers, pulled the cover back and gasped. A young woman lay there, her face pale and lips blue, and Zaylie realized she was chained to the bed. Her eyes were opened slightly, and when Zaylie placed her finger at the girl's neck, she realized she was still alive, but only barely.

Shoving the gun back into her jacket pocket, she kneeled down and said, "Lauren? Can you hear me?"

There was no response. Her skin was as cold as ice, and Zaylie took her jacket off, tucking it and the blanket firmly around the girl's frail body. Suddenly, Lauren's bloodshot eyes flew open wide and she stared at Zaylie, her gaze filled with terror. Zaylie jerked back, startled, just as a large shadow fell over them. With a sinking sense of foreboding, Zaylie realized they weren't alone.

CHAPTER 2

B efore Zaylie could react, a hand grasped the back of her neck and yanked her from the floor. A hard, muscled arm snaked around her waist, pinning her against a solid, firm chest. Zaylie gasped and began to kick her feet, her fingers clawing at the hand that pressed against her throat.

"Curiosity killed the cat," he whispered into her ear, his breath hot against her skin.

His intentions were clear; he was going to kill her.

As he moved his face away from her ear, Zaylie took the opportunity and slammed her head backward, her skull connecting painfully with his chin. With a grunt, he loosened his grasp around her neck, enabling her to release one short scream. Growling, he slammed his fist into her lower back and then clasped her neck in both hands, his grip tightening so painfully that she was unable to move or breathe. Stars exploded in her eyes as she fought to remain conscious, but with each passing second, she could feel the life draining from her body.

God, please help me.

Suddenly, Zaylie heard the sound of frantic scratching, and the back door crashed open. A vicious growl sounded from behind, and she saw a giant, black shadow leap across the room. With a gasp, the man let her go. Zaylie crumpled to the ground, unable to move or speak. Her back throbbed and her head swam wildly, but through the haze, she watched as Smutti took the man down, her teeth bared viscously as she sank them into his neck. He screamed in pain and tried to shove her away, but she wouldn't stop, and the growls that emanated from her throat sent chills down Zaylie's spine.

I need my gun, she thought to herself, her heart sinking when she realized it was in her jacket pocket, and her jacket was across the room on the bed.

The man elbowed Smutti hard in the head, and with a yelp, she jumped back. *He's going to kill us both now,* Zaylie thought, feeling sick to her stomach. Smutti moved to stand over her owner, her body covering Zaylie's protectively. Although Zaylie couldn't see the man, she could hear him slowly rise from the floor, his breathing heavy.

Suddenly, over the pounding in her ears, Zaylie heard voices outside of the cabin. With a grunt, the man turned and raced out the back door, and just like that, it was all over.

Zaylie lay there, unable to move, waiting for them to arrive and help her. She wondered how Lauren was doing, or if she'd even make it. The front door swung open, and Smutti began to growl again.

"Whoa there, girl. I'm not going to hurt either of you."

Zaylie immediately recognized Kaleb's voice and breathed a sigh of relief.

"Smutti, stand down," she forced the words, which were barely just a whisper, past her trembling lips. Smutti reluctantly stepped away, her tail down and ears back. She'd disobeyed her master when Zaylie told her to stay outside. She'd chosen to ignore her training, no matter the consequences, to save Zaylie's life. Zaylie had always known Smutti was special, and in that moment, she knew she couldn't love her more.

The following events passed in a blur. Zaylie had been without oxygen for too long during the struggle, and her back was in so much pain that she could barely move. The trip down the mountain was excruciating, as she had to be carried every step of the way, but all she could think about was Lauren and the man who had kidnapped her. Would she be okay? Would they be able to catch him?

After a few hours, Zaylie was admitted to the hospital and immediately put on oxygen. As soon as the medication the doctor administered started taking effect, she drifted off into a deep sleep.

The next morning, she awoke to the sound of beeping machines and an IV stuck in her arm. The oxygen mask was gone, thankfully, and she glanced to her left to find Gran snoring softly in a chair beside the bed.

"Gran?" she whispered, her throat sore.

Jerking awake with a snort, Gran sat upright and blinked, her glasses a bit smudged. "Zaylie," she exclaimed, jumping to her feet like a teenager instead of the 76-year-old that she was. "How are you feeling?"

"Just peachy," Zaylie said, a smile spreading across her face.

"Don't you play with me, young lady. I've been worried sick," Gran scolded, taking her glasses off to clean them. "I knew you didn't need to be doing this sort of thing."

Ignoring her rant, Zaylie asked, "How is Lauren? Have you heard anything?"

Gran hesitated, and Zaylie felt her chest tighten. "One of the nurses told me she didn't make it," she said, her eyes softening as she reached out to pat her granddaughter's hand. "I'm sorry, honey. At least you were able to find her, though. Otherwise, her parents might have never known what happened to her."

Zaylie took a deep breath, fighting the tears that burned the backs of her eyes. She felt like a failure. Maybe if she'd gone sooner...

"Stop blaming yourself, Zaylie," Gran said gently as if reading her thoughts. "You did your best."

With a sigh, she nodded and asked if the man had been caught.

"No." Gran shook her head. "It's as if he just disappeared. The police have been hanging around, waiting for you to wake up so they could question you about what he looked like."

"I don't know what he looked like." She squeezed her eyes shut and rubbed her forehead. "I didn't see him." Opening her eyes once again, she asked, "How did you get here so quickly?"

"As soon as the police called, I jumped on the first flight I could find," Gran explained, sitting on the bed beside her. "I got here early this morning."

"What about Smutti?" she wanted to know. "Where is she?"

"She's fine," Gran quickly assured her. "Apparently, she refused to leave your side, so they had to sedate her and she's now at a nearby vet. I went by earlier and checked on her, and she's doing just fine."

"Good." Zaylie breathed a sigh of relief.

The doctor entered the room then, and after checking Zaylie's vitals and charts, he said she could leave that afternoon but would need to take it easy for about a week.

"You've got a bad bruise on your back where the man hit you, so you don't want to push yourself too hard just yet," he warned.

After he left the room, Gran cleared her throat and said, "I have an idea."

"Uh oh," Zaylie muttered, grinning.

"Why don't you come back to the island with me for a few weeks while you recover?" she asked, her eyes sparkling with excitement. "You're way overdue for some time off, and you can stay with me at Azalea Bluff."

"Do you think I should be away from the training center that long?" Zaylie asked uncertainly.

"Leslie is a wonderful manager and will do just fine without you for a few weeks," Gran stated, and Zaylie knew she was right. Leslie was not only the manager of Zaylie's search and rescue training center, but she was also a very good friend, and Zaylie knew she could trust her.

She'd just agreed to Gran's plan when another knock sounded on the door and two police officers entered. Zaylie told them everything she could remember, giving her regrets that it wasn't more.

"He wouldn't let me see his face," she said, sighing.

"Could you give us a rough idea of his size?" one of the officers asked.

"He was taller than me," she said, shivering as her mind traveled back to relive the details. "I'm 5'6", and I can still feel the lump on the back of my head where I hit his chin, so I'd say he's around 5'9" or 5'10". He was very strong and muscular, and his voice was deep and raspy, but I think he was intentionally making it sound that way."

"What did his accent sound like? Was it local to the area?"

She hesitated, closing her eyes as she tried to remember exactly how he'd sounded. "I don't believe so," she said slowly. "He had a southern accent, but I don't believe he was from West Virginia."

Nodding, both men stood to their feet and

handed her a card. "If you think of anything else, please give us a call."

The next day, after calling Leslie to fill her in on everything, Zaylie and her grandmother headed south.

CHAPTER 3

As Zaylie, Gran, and Smutti drove from the Savannah airport, Zaylie fidgeted impatiently in the passenger's seat, the pain in her back and neck temporarily forgotten as they headed toward the island. No matter how often she'd visited in the last twenty years, the memories never failed to flood her mind every time she returned to Whisper Island.

After her sister was kidnapped that horrible night so long ago, Zaylie was traumatized so badly that she could barely function afterward. The doctors had to sedate her, but even the sedation didn't stop the nightmares. The police searched for days, and Zaylie remembered how tense and on edge her parents were during those agonizing days of waiting and worrying. When Zoe's body was found by a jogger in the woods near the park, that was her family's final undoing. Her dad decided to join an old high school friend in a new business venture in Tennessee, so they packed up and left the island for good. Zaylie could still remember the heartbreak of having to tell her grandparents, friends, and beloved island goodbye. She'd cried for days afterward.

The business venture, a training center for search and rescue dogs, turned out to be a great success and thankfully kept her father occupied. Her mother, however, drifted further and further away from them. A year after Zoe's death, Arnold Layne's business partner and best friend sold his share of the training center and left...with Zaylie's mother at his side.

Zaylie could still remember the horrible argument her parents had the day her mother left. She'd said she couldn't be around her husband and daughter anymore, that it was too painful. So, she'd walked away, leaving Zaylie to be raised by her father. Zaylie always suspected her mother blamed her for not saving her sister, and Zaylie blamed herself. Why did she let Zoe put her in that closet? And why hadn't she been able to tell the police more about what happened? If she'd insisted on staying by her sister's side, maybe she could have somehow stopped that man from taking her. And if her mind hadn't blocked out the main details of what happened, the police might have been able to find Zoe in time.

After her mother left, Gran and Gramp moved to Tennessee for over a year to help their son-in-law and granddaughter. Although nothing was ever truly normal again, Gran had taken the place of Zaylie's mother and Zaylie adored her. If not for Gran, she wasn't certain she would have made it through those trying teenage years.

When Gran pulled up in front of an old, wrought-iron gate that connected to a stone fence, Zaylie felt her stomach tighten. She'd been back to the island many times in the last twenty years, but she hadn't stepped foot inside Azalea Bluff since Zoe was kidnapped.

"Are you okay, sweetie?"

Gran's concerned voice broke through the fog in Zaylie's brain, and she looked over to smiled uncertainly at her grandmother.

"I think so," she replied softly. "It feels strange to be coming back here after all these years."

After Gramp died last year, Gran took her son-in-law up on his offer to sell her home and move to Azalea Bluff. Although Zaylie's father knew he'd never return to live on the island, he still loved Azalea Bluff and wanted it cared for. He'd hired people throughout the years to keep the place in shape, but Gran was the first to live in the old house in twenty years. Zaylie often wondered why her grandmother wanted to live there by herself, especially after what happened, but she knew the place meant a lot to her. Gran had grown up on the island and was best friends with Dad's aunt, so she had a lot of good memories there.

Gran reached over and patted Zaylie's hand. "Have you told your dad what's going on?"

Zaylie shook her head. "No," she replied. "I haven't talked to him in several days. I'll call him tonight."

After Zaylie's dad remarried a little over a year ago, he'd handed the business over to Zaylie and went traveling with his new wife. They were currently somewhere in Wyoming without much cell phone service, but Zaylie knew she needed to at least try to let her dad know what was going on. Even though their relationship was different now that he had a new life, they were still close and he deserved to hear from her.

After pressing the automatic gate opener, Zaylie and Gran drove through the entranceway, both smiling as they took in the familiar beauty of Azalea Bluff. A quarter-mile-long driveway stretched out before them with giant oak trees lining either side, their moss-draped branches curving overhead to create a beautiful, natural archway. Beams of sunlight forced their way through, bouncing along the road ahead, and Zaylie found herself wishing it was springtime, when the azalea bushes that grew wildly all around were in full bloom, their brilliant colors so beautiful that they could easily take one's breath away.

They came to a bend in the road and followed it around to the left before the road straightened once again, revealing the house just up ahead. It was like Zaylie was stepping into the past as the familiar old place drew closer and closer, but instead of making her feel sad or anxious, it was like seeing a dear old friend again. It was like coming home.

"It's as beautiful as ever," she said with a sigh as they pulled up in front of the house and stopped.

After grabbing the few belongings they'd brought along, the two walked up the four brick steps that led to the porch while Smutti explored the yard. Worn rocking chairs bumped gently back and forth in the breeze, while the swing to the left creaked slightly on its hinges.

Gran unlocked the massive oak front door, and as soon as Zaylie stepped inside, she felt the anxiety start to crash in. For a brief moment, she closed her eyes and forced herself to breathe as she tried to remember the good times. Times when her family's laughter rang down the hall, when life was complete and nothing had changed.

"It's still hard for me sometimes, too," Gran said softly, and Zaylie knew her grandmother missed Zoe just as much as she did.

"Does the pain ever truly go away?" Zaylie asked, opening her eyes to look at her grandmother.

Gran smiled sympathetically and shook her head. "Not entirely," she said. "It gets better, but it's always going to be there. We just have to try to focus on the good times and be thankful for those sweet memories we have of our loved ones."

With tears burning the back of her eyes, Zaylie squeezed Gran's hand and went upstairs without another word. She walked past Zoe's old room without opening the door and went into her own room. As she stood in the doorway and looked around, she was relieved to find that Gran had redecorated. If the room had looked the same, Zaylie wasn't certain she could handle it. The memories were just too traumatic.

The next few hours were spent unpacking and

helping Gran make supper. Or, rather, watching Gran make supper, as she wouldn't hear of Zaylie "overdoing it". Although she wouldn't say so to Gran, Zaylie had to admit that her back was aching, and she felt completely exhausted. After supper, she kissed Gran good night and turned in early.

It was barely past midnight when Zaylie woke up. Rubbing her eyes, she looked at the clock and sighed. What had awakened her? She vaguely remembered having a bad dream, but what the dream consisted of, she wasn't certain. Turning over, she tried to go back to sleep.

Twenty minutes later, she was still awake. With a sigh, Zaylie threw back the covers and climbed out of bed. Smutti sat up in her own bed in the corner and looked at her owner curiously, but Zaylie told her to stay put.

"I'll be back in a few minutes," she whispered as she grabbed a flashlight and tiptoed out into the hallway.

The house was still and quiet, with the ticking of the grandfather clock downstairs the only sound that echoed through the silent home. Zaylie stood still for a moment, trying to shake the feeling of darkness that seemed to envelop the house. She'd always loved it here as a child, but now it felt like the memories might suffocate her. Everywhere she looked, she saw Zoe, and it was like the house was doing everything it could to remind her of what happened there.

After a moment, Zaylie took a deep breath and walked as quietly as a ghost down the stairs and into the kitchen, where she fixed herself a cup of hot lavender tea. As she blew into the steaming mug moments later, she went into the living room to find a book. Clicking on one of the side table lamps, she walked over to the bookshelf and thumbed through several of the old classics until she found "A Tale of Two Cities". It had been a while since she'd read the old Dickens novel, and when she turned to make her way to the sofa, her eyes were drawn to a painting of a beautiful young woman that hung on one of the far walls. Zaylie set the book by the lamp and walked closer to the painting. It had hung on that wall for as long as she could remember, and the shadows cast by the lamp made the woman's emerald green eyes, which looked so much like Zaylie's, almost glow.

Great Aunt Azalea stared back at Zaylie like a woman trapped within the confines of time. She was about eighteen years old when her picture was painted, and no one could argue over how beautiful she was. Her red lips were turned up around the edges in a slight smile, and her rich, auburn hair glistened in the back light, creating a soft glow around her beautiful face. There was something mysterious in her eyes, which perfectly matched the color of her 1960s-style dress. Zaylie had never known her; in fact, neither had her father. According to the vague stories she'd been told, Azalea just disappeared into thin air one day during the summer of…

Zaylie's train of thought was suddenly interrupted when something started niggling in the back of her mind. Frowning, she tried to put together just where her mind had been going. She was thinking of Great Aunt Azalea's mysterious disappearance, but why had that…

Zaylie's eyes widened, and she spun around in search of her phone. Snatching it off the table beside the sofa, she pulled up the article on Lauren's disappearance. When her eyes landed on the date, she could hardly believe it. Lauren disappeared on June the 18th, the same day Zoe was kidnapped.

"Curiosity killed the cat."

Zaylie's shoulders tensed, and she took a step backward, shaking her head. The kidnapper's voice had echoed through her mind unexpectedly, and she now remembered what had awakened her. She'd been having a nightmare about Lauren's killer, but there was something else that she couldn't quite put her finger on…

"I could get away with the moon if I wanted to."

With a gasp, Zaylie dropped the cup of tea, her face draining of all its color as the shattering of glass filled the room. Within seconds, she heard Gran hurrying from the main bedroom.

"Zaylie?" she called out in a frightened voice. She rounded the corner to the living room, and when she spotted her granddaughter, she hurried to her side and asked, "Honey, what's wrong? What's happened?"

Like a zombie, Zaylie slowly turned to look at her grandmother, and in a hoarse whisper, she said, "The man who kidnapped Lauren and...and attacked me. Gran, it's the same man who killed Zoe."

CHAPTER 4

Zaylie didn't sleep for the rest of the night, and at eight o'clock sharp, she was heading out the door to pay Sheriff Harper a visit. Bill Harper had been in charge of Zoe's case twenty years ago and was still the sheriff of Whisper Island. He'd taken it upon himself to continue the search for Zoe's killer for years and had always been willing to help Zaylie in any way he could.

"Stay here with Gran," Zaylie told Smutti as her dog trailed her to the front door. "I'll be back soon."

Zaylie had just reached out for the door handle when Smutti stiffened and let out a sharp bark. She was facing the door, which let Zaylie know someone was approaching. After the night she'd had, Zaylie's nerves were on edge and she immediately felt herself tense. Who would be calling at such an early hour? And how did they get past the front gate?

Grabbing a nearby umbrella to use as a weapon, Zaylie took a deep breath and swung the front door open. A large, navy blue truck was parked in front of the house, and a tall, muscular man around Zaylie's age was walking up the porch steps.

"Ryker?" she asked, blinking in surprise. "What are *you* doing here?"

His hazel eyes sparkled as they swept over her

from head to toe. "It's nice to see you again, too, Zaylie," he replied, smiling.

Zaylie hadn't seen Ryker Steele in nearly twelve years. His twin sister, Rita, was one of her best friends. Ryker, however, was one of her best enemies. When they were little, he'd throw mud at her and intentionally trip her at church. When they became teenagers, he teased her mercilessly and stole her first kiss. She could still remember how furious she'd been when she realized it was *him* behind that Halloween mask and not Micah Pierce.

Cocking an eyebrow, Zaylie stated, "You didn't answer my question. What are you doing here?"

He'd joined the Navy when he was eighteen, and as she hadn't seen him since, she was surprised by how much he'd changed. He was taller than she remembered, and his thin, narrow build had filled out quite nicely. His hair was as black as ever, and he'd let it grow out a bit longer than the Navy typically allowed. Rita talked about him all the time, much to Zaylie's chagrin, but no one had mentioned he was back on the island.

"I'll answer your question as soon as you give me a nice big hug."

The moment Ryker opened his arms and took a step forward, Smutti immediately pushed past her owner and let out a formidable bark.

Blinking, Ryker froze, his arms outstretched like a scarecrow.

"Is it going to eat me?" he wanted to know as he

and Smutti eyed each other warily.

"Only if I give her the signal," Zaylie replied tartly.

Looking back up, Ryker asked, "You wouldn't really do that, though, would you?"

Zaylie shrugged. "That depends."

Ryker raised both his eyebrows. "On?"

"On whether you behave yourself while you're here."

The twinkle came back into Ryker's eyes then and he said, "I'll try, but I can't make any guarantees."

"Well, as long as you try," she replied with a slight smile. Rubbing Smutti behind the ears, she said, "Stop growling, girl. When I want you to hurt him, I'll let you know."

Smutti immediately obeyed the command, but continued to keep a wary eye on their visitor.

"Ryker, is that you?"

Gran's voice rang out from the foyer, and Zaylie opened the door wider to allow Ryker entrance.

"Yes, ma'am," Ryker replied with a charming smile as he stepped inside. "How are you, Mrs. Ferguson? You're looking mighty lovely this morning."

Zaylie had to force herself not to roll her eyes. It seemed Ryker Steele hadn't changed a bit.

"Oh, stop," Gran said with a grin, but Zaylie didn't miss the blush on her cheeks.

"Is anyone going to tell me why he's here?" Zaylie spoke up. "And how he managed to get past the front gate?"

"I gave him the code last week when I asked him to stop by and give me a quote to fix the widow's walk," Gran stated. "I was up there the other day, and the railing is very wobbly."

Zaylie touched her grandmother on the arm. "Gran, what were you thinking? It's too dangerous for you to be up there by yourself."

Gran waved a hand in the air and said, "Phooey. It'll be fine once it's fixed. Ryker, have you had breakfast?"

Ryker shook his head. "No, ma'am, actually I haven't."

"How do blueberry pancakes sound?"

"Scrumptious," he replied with a grin.

Clapping her hands, Gran turned and headed toward the kitchen. "A plate of my famous blueberry pancakes is coming right up," she called over her shoulder.

"Well, while the two of you have a nice cozy breakfast, I've got things to do," Zaylie stated as she grabbed her purse. "See you later, Ryker."

"You still haven't given me that hug," Ryker said, stepping around her to block her exit.

Pursing her lips, Zaylie crossed her arms and asked, "Are you on leave or something? I mean, you're not going to be hanging around here for very long, right?"

A slow grin spread across Ryker's face and he asked, "Didn't Rita tell you? I got out two months ago. I'm back on the island for good."

Zaylie didn't know whether to congratulate him or cry. He'd always been the type who rubbed her the wrong way, and the thought of seeing him more often was not very appealing.

"No, Rita didn't tell me," she replied with a forced smile. "Welcome home, Ryker."

Before Ryker could convince her to give him that hug, she quickly stepped around his large frame and dashed out the front door. She heard Smutti barking and secretly wished she'd nip his leg or something. It wasn't kind to wish that on someone, though. Was it?

Twenty minutes later, Zaylie was being ushered into Sheriff Harper's office. As soon as he spotted her, his face lit up and he hurried over to pull her into a bear hug.

"Zaylie Layne, it sure is good to see you," he said, pulling back to smile down at her.

"It's good to see you, too, Uncle Bill," she replied, calling him by the old nickname she'd given him years ago.

"To what do I owe the pleasure of this visit?" he asked as he motioned for her to sit in one of the chairs opposite his desk.

Zaylie sat down and took a deep breath, a little uncertain of where to begin. When Bill saw the look on her face, he leaned back against his desk and studied her closely.

"Do you remember how I was after Zoe was

taken?" she asked, getting right to the point. When Bill nodded, she continued, "I barely spoke for weeks, and when you asked what I saw and heard that night, all I could tell you was that a man took my sister."

"You were a child, Zaylie," he said gently. "And you were badly traumatized."

Zaylie sighed. "I know, but you'd think that I would have been able to remember *something.* The doctors said I blocked it all out. I think that's one reason Mom blamed me for Zoe's death." Zaylie looked down at her hands and shook her head. "If I'd been able to tell you more about what happened, maybe Zoe would have been found before...before..."

"It wasn't your fault, Zaylie," he interrupted. Tilting his head, he asked, "What's this about? I thought you were finally trying to put all of this behind you."

"I was," Zaylie replied. Standing, she wrapped her arms around her waist and began slowly pacing around the room. "Until last night."

Bill's brow furrowed and he asked, "What happened last night?"

Zaylie turned to face him. "It all came back."

Bill blinked, and he pushed himself off the desk to stand up to his full height. "What do you mean?"

Tucking a strand of auburn hair behind one ear, Zaylie explained what had happened in West Virginia. "It was the same man, Uncle Bill," she told him. "I didn't realize it at the time, but coming back to the island sort of brought it all back, I guess, and last night I had a dream about it. When I woke up, it was like every lost piece in my mind had been put back together and I could clearly hear his voice when he spoke to Zoe that night. It was the same voice I heard in that cabin in West Virginia, and Bill, he took that girl on June the 18th."

Bill's eyes had gotten so big that they looked like two silver dollars staring back at her.

"Zaylie, this is insane," he breathed. "What did he say when he took Zoe?"

Zaylie stopped pacing and sat back down, her hands clutched together in her lap. "Zoe asked him what he wanted, and he said he wanted a lot of things, especially her. When she told him he wouldn't get away with it, he said he could get away with the moon if he wanted to."

While Zaylie spoke, Bill grabbed his phone and recorded everything she said. He also took notes, and when she stopped speaking, he asked, "Can you remember anything else about that night? Did you see him?"

Zaylie shook her head. "Not that I can recall. From what I remember, I could only make out shadows through the slats in the closet door." Looking down at her hands, she squeezed her eyes shut and said, "All I remember after that is Zoe screaming as he dragged her from the house. I...I felt so helpless, Bill. I tried to get out and help her, but she'd locked me inside and I couldn't get out."

Zaylie buried her face in her hands and began to cry as searing pain from the horrible memories swept over her like a tidal wave. Bill immediately came to her side and wrapped his arms around her. He'd always been like a second father to her, and the support of a caring father was what she needed in that moment.

"Even if you had been able to escape from that closet, he only would have taken you, too," he told her. Pulling back, he offered Zaylie a box of tissues from his desk. After she'd blown her nose and wiped her face, he put a finger beneath her chin and forced her to look at him. "Zoe saved your life, honey. She knew you would have tried to help her, which is why she locked you in that closet. She loved you so much."

Trying to gather her emotions, Zaylie blew her nose once again and sat up straighter. "I'd like to review the case again," she told him.

Bill hesitated, his eyes uncertain. "Are you sure you want to put yourself through that again, Zaylie?" he asked. "As much as I hate to say this, remembering what the man said and the sound of his voice isn't much to go on. Unless it was a voice you recognized?"

Zaylie shook her head. "No, I didn't recognize his voice, but I think he may have been disguising it," she said. Looking up at him pleadingly, she said, "For all we know, he might have been doing this for the last twenty years. Or maybe something happened and he's started back, which means others will be killed if he's not stopped. If I go through the files and evidence once again, maybe I'll remember something else that will help us catch him. Please say it's okay, Uncle Bill."

Bill heaved a sigh and nodded. "Okay," he agreed with a bit of reluctance. "All of our old case files have been moved to the basement. I would take you down there myself, but I have an appointment in ten minutes. I'll get one of the boys to take you down there, and as soon as I can, I'll start digging into other murders that have taken place on June the 18th."

Standing, Zaylie hugged Bill again and thanked him. She knew he was concerned about her decision, as she'd decided over two years ago to try to put the past behind her. She'd returned the files to Bill and told him that after ten years of searching for the truth, she just couldn't do it anymore. This time, however, things were different. She could actually remember details now that she couldn't before. Would it make a difference? She wasn't sure, but she knew she had to try.

CHAPTER 5

Bill led Zaylie down a hallway and into a large conference room where a dark-haired, vaguely familiar man in his late thirties sat at one of the tables.

"Zaylie, you remember my nephew, don't you?" Bill asked.

Zaylie blinked in surprise. "Devon?" she asked.

The man smiled and nodded. "That's me," he replied, standing up to shake her hand. "How are you, Zaylie?"

"I'm pretty good," she said. "Wow, how long has it been since I've seen you? Fifteen years?"

Devon tilted his head to the side as he thought it over. "Hmm, probably closer to eighteen."

"Devon and his wife recently moved back to the island," Bill explained. "Devon is a security system technician. He just opened his own business, and he agreed to help us digitize our old case files."

Devon nodded. "Since my business is still new, I have some spare time on my hands," he said. Motioning to the scanner, computer, and stack of boxes on the table, he added, "As you can see, I have my work cut out for me."

"I've got to get going," Bill interrupted. "Devon, will you show Zaylie to the basement?"

"Follow me," Devon told her as Bill hurried from

the room. "What do you need in the basement?"

Zaylie followed Devon back out into the hallway, waving to a couple of familiar faces as they passed by. "I want to go through my sister's case files again," she told him.

Devon glanced down at her in confusion, and then his eyes lit with understanding. "Ah, yes, I remember now," he said as he stopped to open a door at the end of the hall. "Zoe was a few years older than you, wasn't she?"

Zaylie nodded. "Yes, she was fifteen when she... when it happened."

Devon shook his head sympathetically. "That was such a tragedy."

As Devon pushed the basement door open, Zaylie was immediately hit with a dank, musty smell. It seemed obvious that the basement wasn't visited very often.

"Do you remember Zoe?" Zaylie asked after Devon reached inside and flipped on the lights.

"A little," he replied, stepping aside to let Zaylie through the narrow doorway. "I was eighteen at the time, so I guess we ran in different circles. There were a handful of times, though, that we ended up at the same parties. I remember being particularly surprised when she showed up at one of Cameron Sterling's parties. Remember him? He's that rich guy who spent summers here with his family. He actually still has that big house out on the bluff and lives here during the warmer months."

Zaylie stopped and looked back at Devon, her forehead lowering in question. "Parties?" she asked. "I don't remember Zoe attending many parties, especially not Cameron Sterling's wild parties where the older boys were sure to be."

Without answering, Devon glanced at his wristwatch and said, "I'm sorry, Zaylie, but I just remembered I've got a Zoom call with a potential new client. If you go down those steps in front of you and turn to the right, you'll see the room with the old case files. They're all in alphabetical order."

Before Zaylie could respond, Devon spun on his heel and disappeared around the corner. She stood there for a moment, thinking about what he'd said and wondering why he'd so obviously avoided her question. Should she ask Uncle Bill about it? He'd always been rather defensive when it came to his only nephew, so she wasn't certain that was such a good idea.

With a sigh, Zaylie turned and headed down the steps. They led her down into what felt like a large, black hole, and Zaylie stopped to turn on her phone's flashlight. The small, flickering light Devon had clicked on just inside the door quickly faded away as Zaylie went further down, and when she made it to the file room, she fought the feeling of claustrophobia that threatened to suffocate her. Ever since being locked inside that closet, Zaylie had hated tight spaces. Although this wasn't necessarily tight, the ceilings were low and the thought of being underground made her skin crawl. When she spotted a light switch, she quickly flipped on the light and breathed a sigh of relief. The small room was lit by one single, yellow lightbulb, and shadows from the large shelves and filing cabinets seemed to grow bigger and more foreboding by the second.

"Just find Zoe's box and get out of here," she muttered to herself.

There were several shelves in the room labeled "Cold Cases", so finding the "L" boxes wasn't easy. On such a small island, there wasn't much crime, but the department had kept case files dating back over fifty years. Due to the lack of detectives and up-to-date methods, the Whisper police relied on the help of the Savannah police to help with bigger, more involved crimes. Zaylie remembered how dedicated both departments had been when trying to find Zoe's killer. There wasn't much evidence to go on, but as she pulled the box from the shelf, she hoped something inside would further jog her memory.

Zaylie had just pulled the box from its shelf and was heading back toward the stairs when, suddenly, the light went out. She stood there, frozen in place, as her heart immediately began to race. The darkness in the basement was so black and thick that she felt like she was suffocating. Why had the lights gone out? Was there a power outage? Was someone trying to scare her?

Trying to remain calm, Zaylie put the box on the floor and once again pulled her phone from her pocket. Her hands were shaking so badly, though, that the phone slipped from her fingers and skittered loudly across the floor. With a groan, Zaylie got down on all fours and began to feel around the damp, cold ground.

Stay calm, she told herself. *You'll find your phone and be out of here in a matter of seconds.*

But she couldn't find the phone, and the darkness was steadily closing in on her. She tried to control her breathing and stay focused, but the feeling of panic was threatening to overtake her. Should she scream for help? Would anyone even be able to hear her all the way down here?

Just then, Zaylie heard something, and she froze again. Someone was in the basement with her; she could feel their presence like a cold breeze. The hair on the back of her neck stood up, and she began to fight a different kind of panic. Oh, why hadn't she brought Smutti along with her? She would have already led Zaylie out of this black pit, and she'd have known all along if someone else was in the basement with them. Who would be down there? Did they intend to do her harm?

"Zaylie?" a voice suddenly rang out. "Where are you?"

Through the thick haze of fear and panic, Zaylie recognized Bill's voice and blew out a sigh of relief.

"I'm down here," she called out, her voice trembling.

A small beam of light bounced along the walls as the sound of Bill's footsteps drew nearer. He rounded the corner then, and Zaylie saw that he carried a small flashlight.

"Some idiot hit the transformer and cut off the electricity," Bill explained as he hurried to Zaylie's side. "Are you okay? I know how you are about the dark and tight spaces, so I got here as soon as I could."

"Just get me out of here," she said in a breathless tone. "Please."

As Bill grabbed the box and led Zaylie back upstairs, she glanced over her shoulder and wondered what she'd thought she'd heard. Perhaps no one had been there after all; it was probably just her imagination getting the better of her. Or perhaps she'd simply heard Bill coming to her rescue. Either way, she had no desire to go back down into that horrible black hole anytime soon.

CHAPTER 6

As Zaylie was leaving the police station, she was so lost in her thoughts that she didn't see the man walking toward her in the lobby. When she bumped into him and nearly dropped the box she was carrying, she stumbled backward and winced in pain. She was still sore from the attack, and being jarred so roughly wasn't the most pleasant experience.

"Why don't you watch where you're going?" a gruff voice snapped.

"I could say the same to you, mister," she shot back as she moved the box around to balance on one hip.

The man standing before her wore a baseball cap, denim jacket, and a rather unpleasant frown on his face. He looked to be around the age of forty and had a heavy five o'clock shadow which only added to his already rough appearance. His blue eyes were deep set and lined with black circles, but as soon as he got a good look at Zaylie, his features immediately softened and he smiled.

"I'm sorry, Miss Layne," he said. "I didn't realize it was you. Are you alright?"

Zaylie raised her eyebrows in surprise. "Uh, yes, I'm fine," she stammered. "Do...do I know you?"

"Sort of," he replied with a chuckle. Stepping

forward, he held out a hand and said, "I'm Clark Schultz. We met when I delivered a load of supplies to your business a few years ago."

Zaylie thought hard for a moment, and then it struck her. Clark was a truck driver, and he'd delivered some new training supplies to Crescent Moon about three or four years ago. She'd never seen him before and remembered being surprised when he'd told her he lived on the island.

"Oh, yes, I remember now," she replied with a warm smile as she accepted his offered hand. "Do you still drive a truck?"

Clark nodded. "Yes, that's why I'm here. I got a lousy speeding ticket last week that I wanted to talk to Bill about. He said he'd take care of it for me this time as long as I watch my speed from now on."

"I'm glad he was able to help you with it," Zaylie replied, realizing Bill's appointment he'd referred to earlier must have been with Clark. Shifting the box on her hip, she added, "I'll see you around, okay?"

Clark eyed the box curiously for a moment before wishing her a good day. As Zaylie walked to her car, she wondered once again why she'd never seen him on the island before now and made a mental note to ask Gran about it.

She'd just gotten into her car and was driving out of the parking lot when a call from Rita Steele came through.

"Um, why didn't you tell me you were attacked?"

Rita all but yelled as soon as Zaylie answered the phone.

"I was going to," Zaylie quickly assured her best friend. "Everything just happened so fast. Why didn't *you* tell me your annoying brother was out of the Navy and back home?"

"I didn't tell you that?"

Zaylie rolled her eyes. As much as she loved Rita, her friend could be rather self-absorbed and extremely absentminded.

"*No,* you didn't tell me," Zaylie replied emphatically. "He randomly showed up at the house this morning; I thought Smutti was going to kill him."

Rita giggled. "I know," she said. "He texted me a few minutes ago and told me, which is also how I found out about the attack. Are you okay?"

Zaylie told her everything that had happened, including her visit to the police station that morning.

"Zaylie, this is insane!" Rita exclaimed once Zaylie was finished. "What a crazy coincidence that the guy who killed your sister ended up being the same man who kidnapped this other girl you were searching for."

Rita had always been very blunt with her choice of wording, but Zaylie was used to it by now. She also wasn't surprised that her friend immediately believed it was the same man. She'd gotten the feeling that Bill, and maybe even Gran, were both a little uncertain. Rita, however, would believe someone if they said the moon was pink.

"Yeah, I'm a little unnerved about the whole thing," Zaylie said. "After all the time I spent searching for my sister's killer, I just happened to bump into him at a creepy little cabin halfway up a mountain in West Virginia."

"What are you going to do now?" Rita wanted to know.

"I'm going to look through the case files again and see if I can remember something else," she replied. "Hey, do you know Clark Schultz?"

"Who?"

Zaylie explained who he was. "He delivered some supplies to the center a few years ago. I bumped into him today at the police station, literally, and I just wondered if you knew him."

"No, I don't have a clue who he is," Rita replied, and Zaylie could suddenly hear voices yelling in the background. "Have you asked Gran?"

"No, but I will when I get home. Hey, is everything okay over there?"

Rita sighed. "I'm at rehearsal and a couple of the actors are arguing," she replied, and Zaylie could picture her friend rolling her eyes. "You know how dramatic actors can be."

"Yes, I do," Zaylie said, her lips twitching.

Rita was an amazing actor; she'd starred in one of Broadway's biggest shows in Atlanta for the past four years. Zaylie had always known her friend was destined to be on the stage, but the fact that she was calling someone else dramatic made Zaylie want to laugh out loud.

"You know, I'm starting to get tired of it."

Zaylie blinked. "Of *acting*?" she asked, shocked. Getting the part in that Broadway play had been a dream come true for Rita.

"A little," Rita admitted. "It's been an amazing experience, but the older I get, the more homesick I feel."

It took Zaylie a moment to figure out what had brought this on, and then she nodded her head as understanding struck her. Now that Ryker was home, Rita felt the pull to come back as well.

"Well, you could always work at the school as a drama teacher," Zaylie told her friend as she turned onto Azalea Bluff.

"Can you see me trying to teach those sticky little monsters how to act?" Rita giggled.

Zaylie smiled. "True, but you'd be the best one for the job."

"Well, I don't disagree with you there..." Rita's voice faded out as she pulled the phone away from her mouth and yelled, "Okay, I'm coming! Good grief, you don't have to be so bossy."

"The stage calls?" Zaylie asked when her friend returned to the phone.

"Yes, and it seems I must answer," Rita replied. "Call me again soon?"

Zaylie promised she would and then disconnected the call. She pulled up in front of the house and parked, not failing to notice that Ryker was still there. After grabbing the box of Zoe's case files, she hurried inside.

"Zaylie, honey, a letter came in the mail for you," Gran called from the kitchen. "I put it on your bed."

Wondering why anyone would have sent her something to this address, Zaylie went upstairs and into her bedroom. Smutti was there waiting for her, and Zaylie had to show her pet some attention before she could do anything else.

"Okay, that's enough," she said with a laugh when Smutti kept nudging her hand for more belly rubs.

Walking over to her bed, she retrieved the letter and studied the envelope for a moment. The whole thing had been typed, and there was no return address. With a frown, Zaylie opened the envelope and pulled out what appeared to be a newspaper clipping. Unfolding it, Zaylie's eyes widened in surprise when she realized it was a photo of herself and Smutti, and it had come from the front page of a newspaper in West Virginia.

"Heroic Zaylie Layne and her brave dog, Smutti, to the rescue!" the headline read, but that wasn't the main thing that drew Zaylie's attention. In the center of the article was a message written boldly in red marker that said, **"You'll pay for this, just like your sister did."**

Chills swept over Zaylie's body as the newspaper clipping slipped slowly from her ice-cold fingers. So, she was right; the man who attacked her two days ago really *was* Zoe's killer. How did he know where she was, though? Had he been following her these last two days? And how did he get hold of this newspaper clipping?

Her heart pounding, Zaylie grabbed her cell phone and made a reservation on the next flight from Savannah to West Virginia. She was going back there to talk to the police and see if there were any new leads in the kidnapping investigation. She was going to find this man, and no death threat was going to stop her.

CHAPTER 7

After arguing half the night with Gran, Zaylie was on a plane bound for West Virginia the next day. She knew her grandmother was worried for her safety and also about the fact that her body was still healing from the attack, but time was of the essence. She couldn't let this continue to drag on.

It was after seven o'clock when Zaylie arrived in the tiny West Virginia town, so she got a room at the only motel around and forced herself to wait until the next morning to speak with the police.

"Dogs ain't allowed," the lady at the front desk stated as she eyed Smutti with a cocked eyebrow.

"She's a working dog," Zaylie said. Hoping for a favor, she looked at the woman's name tag and added with a sweet smile, "She was even featured on the front page of your newspaper this week, Mrs. Finch."

Pursing her lips together, Mrs. Finch finally gave in, although she wasn't happy about it. Why she would care in a crummy place like this, Zaylie didn't know, but she politely thanked the woman and hurried to her room before she had a chance to change her mind.

"Hopefully we won't have to stay but one night," she said to Smutti moments later as the two walked into the small, stuffy room.

While Smutti sniffed around, Zaylie jumped into the shower. By the time she was finished, the sun had set and the crickets were chirping. After peeking out the window and noticing there were only two vehicles in the parking lot, Zaylie made certain the deadbolt was on the door. There was something about this place that gave her creepy Alfred Hitchcock vibes, and Zaylie didn't want any unwelcome guests sneaking into her room.

After calling Gran to let her know she'd arrived safely, Zaylie went to bed. It had been a long day. Her back was aching, and she was exhausted. It was only a matter of minutes before she drifted off into a deep sleep.

Several hours later, a bright light lit up the room. Zaylie's eyes popped open and she sat up, her mind still muddled from sleep as she looked around. After a moment, she realized the light was coming from outside. Apparently, someone had parked in front of her room and their headlights were shining directly into her window. With a sigh, she slumped back down into bed and threw the blankets over her head.

The room was quiet, and Zaylie could hear Smutti as she rose from her bed in the corner and slowly walked across the room. When a low, guttural growl suddenly broke the silence, Zaylie threw the covers back and sat up again.

"It's okay, girl. There's nothing to…"

Zaylie stopped mid-sentence when she saw what

Smutti was staring at. The large, black shadow of a man stood at the window, and it almost seemed as if he could see right through the curtains and into Zaylie's room. The way he stood there, so still and unmoving, set off warning bells in Zaylie's mind. Before she could figure out what to do, however, the shadow moved away and she breathed a sigh of relief.

"Smutti, calm down," she said when her dog continued to growl. "He's gone."

With a yawn, she stood up to go to the bathroom when a strange rattling suddenly caught her attention. Stopping dead in her tracks, she turned to face the door, her heart pounding when she saw that the doorknob was slowly being twisted back and forth. Someone was trying to get into her room.

Smutti's growls turned into vicious barks, and she began jumping ferociously at the door. A sudden, loud *bang* vibrated the whole room, and Zaylie realized the man was pounding against the door just as fiercely as Smutti was. The dog wouldn't be scared off, though; she continued, undeterred, in her defense of her master and what she considered to be her territory. With trembling hands, Zaylie hurried back to the bed and grabbed her cell phone with the intent of calling the police. Would they answer in time? And if so, would they be able to get here before the man ripped the door off its hinges and came in after them?

Just then, the rattling and pounding ceased.

Smutti stopped barking and backed away from the door, her whole body stiff as she waited and listened. Zaylie did the same, but the pounding of her heart was drowning out the eerie silence. Suddenly, the headlights from the car shut off, and the room was bathed in darkness. The sound of a car as it drove away could be heard, and then all was silent once again.

Still clutching her phone, Zaylie took a deep breath and slowly moved across the room to stand at the window. The quivering of her hand bounced through the darkness like the static on a TV, but when Zaylie moved the curtain back and looked out, there was nothing to see. There was no car parked in front of her room, and the shadow of the man was long gone.

The next morning, Zaylie marched into the front office to ask about the incident the night before. The same woman was at the front desk, and she looked even grumpier this time.

"We've only got one other guest, and they ain't complained about hearing any noises," Mrs. Finch snapped when Zaylie told her what happened.

"Would you mind if I asked them about it?" Zaylie wanted to know.

"They're already gone," the woman stated with a sniff. "They left just before sunrise."

Zaylie sighed with frustration. "Well, what about camera footage? Could I see that?"

Mrs. Finch's lip curled with annoyance. "We've only got the one camera, and it's pointed here at the office, so you wouldn't be able to see anything if you tried. Look, lady, we ain't never had such a crazy complaint before, and if this is the kind of trouble you bring, maybe you should take your dog and leave town."

"As much as I'd love to do so," Zaylie said, her jaw clenched, "I'm afraid I can't leave this charming little place just yet."

As Zaylie drove to the police station, she fumed at how rude that woman had been. And what kind of place didn't have cameras? Zaylie almost wondered if the woman knew more than she was letting on, but then thought with a smirk that she probably wasn't that intelligent. She then felt guilty for thinking something so mean.

Ten minutes later, she entered the tiny police station and immediately spotted the two officers she'd met before.

"Miss Layne," Officer Peterson said as he stood up in surprise. "I thought you'd left town?"

Officer Turner looked in her direction and raised his eyebrows questioningly.

"I received this in the mail the day before yesterday." Zaylie laid the newspaper clipping on Peterson's desk.

Turner came over to peer over Peterson's shoulder, and after reading the message, they both looked up at her with wide eyes.

"Miss Layne, you need protection," Turner said

in a serious tone.

"What I need is to find this guy," she replied. "How is the investigation going?"

Peterson sighed. "The FBI came out and did a thorough search of the cabin and surrounding area," he said. "They couldn't find a thing. This guy knows what he's doing."

"He killed your sister?" Turner leaned against Peterson's desk and crossed his arms as he eyed Zaylie curiously.

Zaylie nodded. "Twenty years ago, to the exact day," she stated. "I didn't realize it was the same man until I went back home and started remembering details I thought I'd forgotten. When I received the newspaper clipping and threatening message, I knew I needed to come back here. Could someone possibly take me up to the cabin? I'd like to have a look around."

Both officers shook their heads. "No, I'm sorry," Turner told her. "Our local church was burned to the ground two nights ago, and we think it was arson. Sheriff Haynes told us we have until the end of the week to get it solved, so I'm afraid we just don't have time to take you up there."

Zaylie nodded. "I understand." Grabbing a pen and piece of paper, she jotted down her number and said, "Look, if you receive any information at all on the case, will you let me know?"

Both men promised they would, and Zaylie left the station. As she and Smutti walked back to the rental car, Zaylie heard her name being called.

Surprised, she turned to find Kaleb, the volunteer who'd helped search for Lauren, jogging toward her.

"Miss Layne, I thought that was you," he said when he reached her side. "What are you doing here?"

Zaylie started to show him the newspaper clipping and explained everything, but decided to hold her tongue at the last second. He may have helped her search for Lauren and then led the police to the cabin in the nick of time, but he was still a stranger.

"I wanted to go back to the cabin and look around," she told him. "The police can't go with me, so I guess I'll just go by myself. If, that is, I can find it."

There was curiosity in Kaleb's eyes, but he didn't question her. Instead, he said, "I can take you if you like."

Zaylie blinked in surprise. "Oh, well..." she hesitated, feeling a little uncertain. Should she go to such a desolate place with a man she barely knew? If not, could she really find it on her own? After a moment, she sighed and said, "That would be great. Thanks, Kaleb."

It took nearly thirty minutes to reach the area where Lauren and her family were camping. Zaylie and Kaleb left their vehicles parked there and began hiking toward the spot where Lauren disappeared.

"Were you raised in this area, Kaleb?" Zaylie

asked as they walked.

Kaleb nodded. "I was," he replied. "My dad left us when I was twelve, and my two older brothers moved away when we were in our twenties."

Zaylie found it a bit odd that he'd shared that particular bit of information with her. Stepping over a fallen tree branch, she asked, "What do you do for a living?"

Kaleb glanced down at her with a slight smile. "You ask a lot of questions, don't you?" When she simply shrugged sheepishly and smiled in return, he faced the trail again and said, "I'm a technician. I travel around to different machine shops and fix broken down equipment."

Zaylie wasn't surprised, as she'd noticed the scars and what appeared to be permanent grease stains on his hands. She glanced over at him, noting the firmness of his jaw and the way his dark eyes seemed to constantly shift around, taking in his surroundings. He wasn't necessarily what one would call handsome, but he was still attractive in a way with his dark, curly hair and muscular physique.

The further they went up the mountain, the quieter Zaylie and Kaleb became. Smutti seemed to remember the area also, and Zaylie noticed how cautious and wary she'd become. When they finally reached the cabin, all three stopped and stared at it in silence for a moment, as if the killer might still be inside.

"You okay?" Kaleb asked softly.

Zaylie took a deep breath and nodded. "Yes," she replied. Bending, she gently rubbed Smutti's back as a way to reassure her. "Come on, girl," she said. "Let's see what we can find."

The three walked forward, across the grass, and up the wooden steps. Kaleb pushed the door open, and as Zaylie stepped inside, she immediately looked at the cot in the corner. She could still see Lauren's frail body lying there so still and quiet, and she rubbed her arms, warding off a sudden chill.

The floorboards creaked beneath their feet as they moved around the small cabin, and it was plain to see the police and FBI had recently been there. Everything was swept clean, the smell of chemicals still weighed heavily in the air, and a snippet of police tape had been left on the floor.

"Feels like a tomb in here," Kaleb commented.

Zaylie nodded in agreement but didn't say anything. She already felt discouraged and wondered why she'd been so determined to come back here. What had she expected to find that the FBI would have overlooked?

With a sigh, she carefully searched the closets and cabinets but knew there was nothing to find. She was just about to suggest they leave when Smutti whined and began digging at the floor in one of the corners near the cot. Her brow furrowing curiously, Zaylie hurried to her dog's side and bent down.

"What is it, girl?" she asked as she grabbed a

small flashlight from her pocket. Reaching down, she felt along the floor where Smutti was digging, and her heart caught when she realized one of the floorboards was loose.

"Did she find something?" Kaleb asked as he moved across the room to stand behind Zaylie.

"I'm not sure," Zaylie said with a grunt as she pulled at the floorboard with her fingers. When it popped loose, she shined the flashlight inside, her eyes widening when she spotted a crumpled-up piece of paper.

"Whoa, what is that?" Kaleb asked as he bent down next to Zaylie.

Zaylie put on a pair of gloves and pulled the paper from its hiding place. Making certain to be careful, she slowly unfolded the paper and held it up to the light.

He's tall and muscular. Constantly hums "I only have eyes for you". -L

Zaylie stared at the scratchy handwriting, her heart pounding. Slowly raising her eyes to meet Kaleb's, she said, "I think we just found a note from the grave."

Kaleb's eyes narrowed. "What do you mean?"

"I believe Lauren wrote this note and hid it before she died."

CHAPTER 8

As soon as Zaylie and Kaleb arrived back in town, they immediately went to the police station. When Turner and Peterson saw them, Zaylie could clearly see the annoyance written on their faces.

"Look at what we found," Zaylie said, placing the plastic bag containing the note on Turner's desk.

Holding up the bag with a sigh, Turner glanced at the note, his eyebrows pulled down into a frown. "I don't understand," he said after reading the note. "What is this, and what does it mean?"

"We found it inside the cabin, hidden beneath a loose floorboard near the cot," Zaylie explained. "I believe Lauren wrote it."

Peterson, who'd been ignoring them until now, rose from his desk and hurried over to see what all the commotion was about.

"You expect us to believe the two of you found this after the FBI already did a thorough search of the place?" Turner asked in disbelief.

While Kaleb explained how Smutti was the one who led them to the location of the note, Peterson quietly walked to a nearby filing cabinet and began digging through a stack of files. After a moment, he pulled out a piece of paper and brought it back to Turner's desk.

"This is the note Lauren left her family the morning she disappeared," he said, placing both notes side by side.

The two officers studied the handwriting on both notes, and after a moment, they looked at each other and then at Zaylie and Kaleb.

"You're right," Peterson said, his eyes wide. "The handwriting on the second note is more hurried, but it's the same. Lauren left us a clue."

"Is there really that much to go on, though?" Kaleb asked.

"We'll have it checked for fingerprints; hopefully, the killer handled the paper before Lauren got it," Turner replied. "Good work, you two."

After insuring they would let her know if they found anything, Zaylie said her goodbyes and left the station.

"Want to grab a coffee?" Kaleb asked.

Zaylie was a bit surprised but politely accepted the offer. As they made their way across the street to the only coffee shop in town, Kaleb suddenly stopped, his eyes narrowing. Zaylie looked to see what he was staring at, her gaze landing on a man that was slowly walking their way. He wore a dirty jean jacket, and his shaggy black hair looked as if it hadn't been washed in weeks. A heavy five o'clock shadow dusted his face, and by his shabby appearance, Zaylie couldn't tell his age.

"Uh, I'm sorry, but I'm going to have to skip out on coffee," Kaleb told her. As he hurriedly began walking toward the man, he turned back to her and called, "Maybe I'll see you later. You're not leaving 'til morning, right?"

Zaylie nodded, and as she and Smutti continued on their way, she couldn't help but notice how tense Kaleb suddenly seemed. When he grabbed the other man by the arm and dragged him into a shaded corner, Zaylie watched them for a moment. It appeared the two were involved in a pretty heavy argument, and Zaylie wondered what it was all about.

That night, as Zaylie got ready for bed, she made certain her gun was out of her suitcase and lying on the table beside her bed. If she was faced with another episode like the night before, she was going to be prepared.

"Wow, what a day this has been," she said with a yawn as she rubbed Smutti's back. "I'm pooped. How about you, girl? You sure did a good job today."

Smutti glanced up at her owner, her golden eyes steady and calm. She'd been by Zaylie's side since she was a puppy, and she seemed to always know exactly what Zaylie was saying. Sometimes, Zaylie thought the dog could even tell what she was thinking.

With a small yawn of her own, Smutti nuzzled Zaylie's hand with her nose as if to said, "You did good today, too," and then went to curl up in her bed.

After Zaylie took a shower, she was about to turn in early when she realized she was out of toilet paper. She tried to call the front desk and ask for more, but no one answered. With a sigh, she slipped into her bathrobe and hurried outside. She was halfway to the front office when she heard the sound of a coyote crying in the distance. Shivering as the cool night air swept over her, she realized just how dark and desolate the area was and thought she probably should have brought the gun along with her. Just in case.

When she reached the office, the sound of raised voices suddenly met her ears. Before she could figure out what was going on, the door swung open, nearly knocking Zaylie down. Stumbling backward, she grabbed a nearby post for support, and her eyes widened in surprise when the same man she'd seen earlier stomped out. His dark, stormy gaze glanced over her, but he didn't say a word as he stalked away. Not wishing to hang around outside in the dark, Zaylie hurried into the office and quickly shut the door behind her.

"What now?"

Raising her eyebrows, Zaylie turned to find that Mrs. Finch, once again, was running the front desk. Did the woman own the place and operate it entirely by herself? *She probably can't find anyone who wants to work for her,* Zaylie thought.

"Good evening, Mrs. Finch," Zaylie said in a forced, friendly tone. "Is everything okay?"

"What do you mean?" she asked, her eyes narrowing.

Pointing toward the front door, Zaylie said, "That man nearly knocked me over the way he came storming out of here just now."

Mrs. Finch rolled her eyes. "Barley Bates is like an annoying little fly that you want to smash with a fly swatter," she stated sneeringly. "Just don't pay any attention to him."

Zaylie tilted her head. "Bates? Is he related to Kaleb Bates?" she wanted to know.

Mrs. Finch nodded. "Yes, he's Kaleb's brother."

Zaylie blinked in surprise. "I thought Kaleb said both his brothers had moved away," she said.

"His two older brothers did," Mrs. Finch replied. "Barley is his younger brother."

Zaylie really wanted to ask why he was at the hotel and what they'd been arguing about, but by the annoyed expression on Mrs. Finch's face, she knew there was no need.

"Could I have a roll of toilet paper?" she asked. "I'm out."

With pursed lips, Mrs. Finch retrieved a roll of toilet paper from the back and placed it on the desk with a firm *thump.*

"You're leaving tomorrow?" she asked, and Zaylie knew the woman was ready to be rid of her and Smutti.

"Yes, ma'am." Zaylie nodded and picked up the toilet paper, adding as she walked out, "Thank you for this."

As she hurried back to her room, Zaylie searched the dark parking lot for Barley Bates, but he was nowhere to be seen. Just as she arrived back to her room and opened the door, however, a sudden chill swept up her spine and she quickly glanced over her shoulder. There, through the darkness, stood Barley Bates. He was leaning against a nearby tree, and his piercing dark eyes seemed to stare right through her. Zaylie stood there for a moment and stared right back, wishing she knew what he was up to. Could he be the one who tried to break into her room last night? And why hadn't Kaleb mentioned he had a younger brother still living in the area? There was something very strange about the whole situation.

When Barley leaned forward and spit out a stream of chewing tobacco, Zaylie went inside her room and closed the door, securely locking it behind her.

CHAPTER 9

O nce Zaylie's plane landed in Savannah, she and Smutti were walking from the airport when a familiar voice called out to her. Surprised, she turned to find Misty Raven waving to her from her car.

"What a small world it is," Zaylie stated with a wide smile as she leaned down to look through the open passenger-side window. Misty's massive St. Bernard mix, Wally, was in the back seat, and he eagerly poked his head around to lick Zaylie's hand

"I was thinking the same thing," Misty said, her gray eyes sparkling. "Are you here to visit your grandmother?"

"Sort of," Zaylie said hesitantly as she motioned for Smutti to sit down. When Misty tilted her head curiously, she explained what had happened the last few days. "I feel like this is it, Misty. I plan to truly find Zoe's killer this time."

Misty's eyes were filled not only with sympathy but also understanding. "I believe in you, Z," she said. "If I was able to find the answers to my past, I know you'll be able to do the same."

"Thank you, Misty," Zaylie said with a warm smile. "Hey, how are things going at the inn?"

"It's hard work, but I'm enjoying it," she replied, proceeding to fill Zaylie in on life in Shady Pines. "I actually just dropped off my aunt and uncle," she said. "They came down from Pennsylvania to visit for a few days."

"I am so happy for you, Misty," Zaylie told her friend. "You searched long and hard for your family."

Misty nodded. "I sure did," she stated with a sigh. "Hey, call me soon and let's meet up for lunch, okay?"

Zaylie promised that she would, and as she watched her friend drive away, she felt more hopeful about finding her own answers. Since Misty was raised in the foster system with no previous records to follow, she'd had to start from scratch to find her family. She'd searched for years and encountered many obstacles along the way, but she'd never given up. She and Zaylie first met a few years ago in Savannah, and they'd immediately hit it off. Now, Misty lived about thirty minutes away in the small town of Shady Pines.

If Misty can do it, then so can I, Zaylie thought as she squared her shoulders and headed to her car.

Once she arrived back at Azalea Bluff, Gran hurried out to greet her. "How did it go?" she asked as Zaylie let Smutti out of the back seat.

As they walked into the house, Zaylie filled her in on everything. She'd just stepped through the front door when she stopped and sniffed the air.

"What's that smell?" she asked.

Gran hesitated and then said with a smile, "Oh,

Ryker has been doing some work on the house."

Zaylie frowned. "I thought he was just going to fix the widow's walk?" she asked.

"While he was here, I asked him to fix a few more things," Gran explained. "The living room and kitchen need a fresh coat of paint. There are also a few boards on the back deck that need replacing, and the list just goes on."

"Is he a contractor now or something?" Zaylie wanted to know. "I don't remember him being especially good with a hammer."

"Oh, yes, now that he's no longer in the Navy, he's doing contracting," Gran replied. "Isn't that wonderful?"

Zaylie eyed her grandmother suspiciously. "Why is that so wonderful? The island already has a contractor."

Gran frowned at Zaylie and stated, "Well, we're certainly big enough to support *two* contractors. Besides, I think it's wonderful to see a young man who is willing to work hard. It just lets me know that my thoughts about Ryker's character were right all along."

Zaylie raised her eyebrows in disbelief. "Are we talking about the same Ryker who used to toilet paper cars and cheat on his history tests at school? He stayed in the principal's office more than he did in an actual classroom."

Gran waved a hand through the air. "He was a child then, Zaylie. Good grief, give the poor man a break," she said with a disapproving shake of her head. "I think he's turned into a very nice young man. And quite a handsome one, too, don't you think?"

"What is this all about, Gran?" Zaylie asked, her green eyes narrowing. "You're not up to your old matchmaking schemes again, are you?"

Gran blinked and rested a hand on her chest dramatically. "Zaylie Layne, I don't know what you're talking about," she stated. "And how dare you call them "schemes". I've never schemed a day in my life."

Zaylie rolled her eyes. "I guess it wasn't "scheming" when you tried to set me up with that new neighbor who turned out to be on the run from the law?"

Gran pursed her lips and said indignantly, "He said he was a doctor! How was I supposed to know he was lying?"

"And what about the schoolteacher who was married and had three children?" Zaylie asked wryly.

"I'd forgotten about that one," Gran muttered. "He seemed like such a nice man."

Zaylie patted Gran on the arm and said, "When I'm ready to settle down, I'll find my own husband. Okay?"

With a sniff, Gran said, "Perhaps," and then hurried away toward the kitchen before Zaylie could protest further.

Shaking her head, Zaylie took her overnight bag upstairs and changed her clothes. During her flight home, she'd written down everything that had happened in the last few days and made a list of people she wanted to talk to. First, she planned to question Devon further about those parties he'd mentioned before. After that, she thought she might pay Cameron Sterling a visit. She barely knew the man, as he was several years older and they'd always run in different circles due to his family's extreme wealth. After Devon had mentioned him, though, it seemed that Zaylie could remember overhearing one of her sister's telephone conversations a few weeks before she died. She'd been talking to one of her friends, and Cameron's name was brought up. Had Zoe had a crush on him? Zaylie couldn't remember what Zoe said, but she remembered who her sister was talking to, and Devon Harper's wife, Erica, was also on the list.

When Zaylie arrived at the police station, Bill told her Devon was installing a new alarm system in someone's home.

"I believe he'll be back here tomorrow to continue working on digitizing those case files," Bill said.

Thanking Bill, Zaylie headed to Devon's house in the hope that his wife would be home.

"Zaylie Layne, is that you?" Erica Harper asked in surprise when she opened the front door to their small, one-story house ten minutes later.

"Hi, Erica," Zaylie said with a smile. "It's been a long time. How are you?"

Beckoning for Zaylie to come inside, Erica said, "I'm good; just trying to settle back into the quiet island life. Would you like something to drink?"

Zaylie declined, and the two sat down in the living room. While Erica jabbered on about moving back to the island, Zaylie glanced around the room. There was a picture on the mantle of Erica and Devon standing next to a young man wearing a graduation cap and gown, and when Zaylie pointed it out, Erica beamed with pride.

"That's our son," she explained. "He graduated from high school last year and is going to college now. We're so proud of him, but I'll admit it's hard when the nest is empty once again."

Once again? If Zaylie remembered correctly, Erica hardly knew what it was to have an empty nest in the first place. She'd gotten pregnant during her senior year of high school, and she and Devon got married right after graduation.

"He's a very nice looking young man," Zaylie told her with a smile.

Erica nodded, and then she looked at Zaylie with serious eyes and said a bit hesitantly, "So, Devon tells me you've started investigating Zoe's death again."

"Yes, I have," Zaylie replied with a nod of her own. "Speaking of Devon, he mentioned that Zoe went to a few parties back in the day. I, of course, was too young to know anything about that, but I was hoping you could tell me more?"

Erica sighed, her eyes softening. "Ah, yes, those were the days," she said with a chuckle. "Zoe didn't care a lick about going to those parties, but I begged her to go with me. I thought I was grown, you know, and wanted to hang out with the older boys."

"Whose parties did y'all go to?" Zaylie wanted to know.

"One was at the beach," Erica replied, "and the others were at Cameron Sterling's house while his parents were away. His parties were the craziest, with a lot of drinking and, well, other things."

"Did Zoe participate?" Zaylie asked, her stomach clenching at the thought of two fifteen-year-old girls going to such wild parties. She knew Zoe would have had to sneak out; their parents never would have allowed her to go if they'd known. She never would have thought of her sister to be the kind of girl to sneak out in the middle of the night to be a part of such a crowd, but perhaps Zaylie had been too young to really know her sister.

"No." Erica shook her head. "She only went because I asked her to, but when we left that last party at Cameron's, she told me she wasn't doing it anymore. I had a wild crush on Cameron, but he kept coming on to Zoe, so I was more than happy for her to stay home. Especially after what happened." Sighing, Erica said in a sad tone, "Zoe was my best friend, but I let childish jealousy get in the way of that. If only I could go back, I never would have talked her into going to those parties."

Ignoring Erica's last statement, Zaylie leaned forward and said, "You mentioned that something happened at Cameron's last party. What did you mean?"

Erica blinked, and the faraway look in her eyes was suddenly replaced with wariness. "Oh, uh," she stammered. "Cameron got a little rough with her, and Zoe flipped out."

Zaylie's brow lowered. "What did he do?" she demanded.

Erica shifted uncomfortably in her seat. "He got drunk and was a little too hands-on with her, so she slapped him."

Zaylie could tell that wasn't all. "And?" she pressed.

Erica glanced down at her hands and muttered, "He slapped her back."

Zaylie started shaking all over as anger and waves of emotion flooded over her. In that moment, she wanted nothing more than to drive over to Cameron Sterling's mansion and give him a piece of her mind. She'd only seen the man a few times, but his obvious arrogance was written all over him. His family was filthy rich, and as far as she knew, he'd never married. She supposed he had no need for the commitment of marriage.

Seeing the look on Zaylie's face, Erica quickly said, "He didn't mean it, Zaylie. Like I said, he was drunk and wasn't thinking."

Zaylie's eyes widened incredulously, and she

asked, "Why are you defending him?"

Erica sat up straighter. "Because I know Cameron," she snapped, "and I don't believe he intended to hit her."

Biting her tongue to keep from snapping back, Zaylie cleared her throat and asked, "Have you seen Cameron since y'all moved back? I heard he lives here during the warmer months."

"Yes, I've seen him a couple of times," Erica stated. Standing, she forced a smile and said, "Well, I hate to rush you off, but I've got some errands to run. It was nice to see you, Zaylie."

Apparently, Erica didn't care to "visit" any longer, and Zaylie said her goodbyes. As she left the Harper house, her mind was filled with thoughts of her conversation with Erica. She'd been Zoe's closest friend, but seeing how she'd reacted just then about Cameron really surprised Zaylie. Erica said she'd had a crush on him when she was a teenager, but in Zaylie's opinion, she acted as if she still did.

Zaylie drove out to the Sterling estate and parked at the gate, gazing in through the iron slats at the mansion just up ahead. She pressed the intercom button and asked to see Cameron, but was told he was out of town. It was just as well, as she was probably still too upset to speak to him after what Erica had just told her. Was Cameron a violent person? Erica seemed to think not, but what kind of man slapped a young girl after being rejected? At only eighteen or nineteen, he'd been young himself, but the tendencies had still been there and Zaylie couldn't help but wonder if Cameron Sterling wasn't the type of man to cross. If she ever had the chance to speak with him, she'd have to make certain to use caution.

CHAPTER 10

The next morning, Zaylie awoke to the loud, high-pitched sound of a drill. She'd stayed up past midnight the night before, going over Zoe's case, and her eyes were barely able to focus as they popped open. Rolling over, she peered across the room and groaned; it was seven o'clock in the morning, and apparently Ryker was already working downstairs.

Scowling, she climbed from the bed and threw on her robe, wincing when her back protested at the sudden, jerky movements. Moving more carefully, she headed downstairs, not giving a second thought to how she must look. She stepped into the living room, hands on her hips as she glared across the room at the man whose back was to her.

"Ryker!" she yelled, attempting to be heard over the noise of the electric drill. "Ry..." she'd just raised her voice again for a second try when he switched the drill off, and her voice reverberated throughout the room in a most embarrassing way.

Brows raised in surprise, Ryker turned to look at her, his eyes surveying Zaylie's wrinkled pajamas, half-tied robe, and mussed hair.

"Well, well, well," he said, his lips twitching in amusement. "I see that beauty herself made it back home…or should I say beast?"

His looks may have changed, but he was still a smart aleck.

"I tend to look better when I haven't been startled out of bed at the crack of dawn," she stated dryly.

"Bad night, huh?" he grinned. "Sorry, Zaylie, but Mrs. Louella hired me to do a job, and after being in the military, I always get an early start."

Crossing her arms, she asked with a yawn, "So, I'm guessing there's no possible way you could come back around noon?"

"Nope, and if I'd known you were going to greet me in such a nice and…*attractive* way, I'd have come even earlier," he said with a smile, his hazel eyes twinkling.

"I don't think either of us would be happy if you'd come any earlier," she stated, brow cocked.

Ryker laughed, and with a sigh, Zaylie gave it up and asked if he would like some coffee.

"I appreciate the offer, but your grandmother has already seen to that," he replied.

"Where is she?" Zaylie asked, looking around. She'd forgotten Gran always got up so early.

"She went to the grocery store." He shook his head, snickering. "That woman has more energy than a five-year-old."

Yes, she did, and at the moment, Zaylie felt she could use a bit of that energy herself. Turning, she went into the kitchen to pour herself a cup of coffee, adding a heaping teaspoon of honey and creamer. She sipped on it as she walked back upstairs to see about Smutti. When she walked outside with her dog, she was surprised to find the air was filled with a thick fog.

I hope Gran will be okay driving in this, she thought worriedly.

After taking Smutti back into the house and feeding her breakfast, Zaylie returned to the living room with Smutti at her heels.

"Ryker, do you know much about Cameron Sterling?" she asked.

Ryker glanced at her curiously. "I did some work on one of his downstairs bathrooms a couple of weeks ago," he replied. "He's not the type to be overly friendly with someone who's working on his house, but I've heard rumors about him."

"What kind of rumors?" Zaylie asked as she sat down on the sofa to nibble on a blueberry muffin. Smutti rested at her feet, making certain to keep a watchful eye on Ryker.

"That he's taken over the family business and made even more money than his father did," Ryker replied as he continued taking the light switch covers off. "I've heard he's been pretty cutthroat, though."

Zaylie tilted her head to one side. "How so?"

"By firing some of the top people who'd been there for years," Ryker replied. "Apparently, one of them tried to sue but then dropped the lawsuit after the brakes in his car mysteriously went out."

Zaylie's eyes widened. "You think Cameron did

that?"

"I don't think someone like that ever does the actual dirty work himself," Ryker stated with a chuckle. "But who knows? None of these rumors may really be true."

"What about his personal life?" Zaylie questioned.

"I don't have to know the man to see that he's a regular Casanova. I was at his house for a week, and as you know, I get an early start," Ryker said. "On three separate mornings, I bumped into three different women leaving his house, and one of them had a busted lip."

Zaylie's mouth dropped open. "Was...was it anyone we know?"

Ryker shook his head. "No, I've never seen any of them before." Glancing at Zaylie, he asked, "Why all the interest in Cameron Sterling?"

Zaylie told him about her visit with Erica the day before. "It's hard for me to picture my sister blatantly disobeying our parents' rules and sneaking out to go to some wild party," she said with a frown.

"Sounds to me like Erica Harper was a bad influence," Ryker commented. "Because from what I remember, your sister had a good head on her shoulders."

Zaylie looked at him in surprise. "You remember her?"

"I was ten when she died, Zaylie, not two," Ryker stated with a slight chuckle. "Of course, I remember her."

"You might have been ten, but you *acted* like you were two," Zaylie returned, rolling her eyes.

Ryker grinned. "I guess you probably still think that about me, huh?"

"I haven't been around you enough yet to decide," she replied with a sniff.

"Well, we'll just have to fix that, won't we?" Ryker asked slyly.

With a moan, Zaylie asked, "Do we have to?" At the expression on his face, she laughed and added, "I'm only kidding. So, what made you decide to get out of the Navy?"

"I missed the quiet island life," he replied with a shrug. "All I wanted when I was eighteen was to get away from this place and live a more exciting life. Now that I'm older and through with all of that, I decided I was homesick." Putting down his drill, Ryker picked up a screwdriver and stared down at it for a moment, a thoughtful expression in his hazel eyes. "After all the fighting and killing and nearly being killed myself a few times," he said softly, "I realized a more simple life wasn't so bad after all."

Zaylie hadn't realized how bad it must have been for Ryker. Rita, in her typical way, rarely talked about anyone but herself, so Zaylie hadn't known he'd nearly been killed.

Just then, Smutti stood up and barked, her tail wagging as she hurried toward the front door.

"Gran must be back," Zaylie said as she headed

outside to help her grandmother carry in the groceries. To her surprise, Ryker did the same.

"Zaylie, good grief, you look like the bride of Frankenstein," Gran exclaimed in horror when she saw her granddaughter's appearance. Glancing at Ryker with an embarrassed smile, she added, "She normally doesn't look so frightful."

"Thanks a lot, Gran," Zaylie stated drolly as she grabbed a couple of grocery bags from the trunk.

Smutti followed them all into the kitchen, and Zaylie watched as Ryker bent over to pet her. He slowly held out his hand, which Smutti sniffed suspiciously, and Zaylie was a little surprised when she slowly began to wag her tail.

"I think she's decided she likes you," Zaylie said with a smile.

"What can I say?" Ryker shrugged, grinning as he rubbed Smutti behind the ears. "I'm just a likable kind of guy."

"So you keep telling me," Zaylie quipped.

Just then, Zaylie's cell phone rang, and she quickly answered when she saw it was Uncle Bill.

"Zaylie, are you back in town?" he asked in a tense tone.

"Yes, I got back yesterday," she replied.

"Thank God," he breathed. "A little girl went missing at the fort this morning. Can you bring Smutti out ASAP?"

Zaylie nodded. "Be there in ten minutes."

"Great," he said. "Zaylie, we don't know for sure, but she might have been kidnapped."

CHAPTER 11

What's wrong?" Gran asked when Zaylie disconnected the call.

Zaylie quickly explained as she rushed from the kitchen. "I've got to hurry," she said. "If she wasn't kidnapped and just wandered off, the fort ruins can be dangerous for an unattended young child. And in this fog, it's even worse."

"I'll go with you," Ryker called from the kitchen.

After quickly changing her clothes and pulling her hair into a ponytail, Zaylie grabbed Smutti's leash and the three headed out. Due to the fog, Ryker had to drive slowly, and Zaylie sat quietly in the passenger seat, her stomach in knots. Had the child really been kidnapped? How old was she? Could it possibly be the same man?

When they finally arrived at the fort, Zaylie quickly hooked Smutti's leash to her collar. She often let the dog work off the lead, but it was too dangerous this time. As the three hurried toward the police car and a small group of people, Zaylie immediately spotted the girl's mother just by the frantic look on the woman's face.

"Tell me what happened," Zaylie said when she reached Bill's side.

"Mrs. Palmer works here at the fort," he told her, his expression taut. "Her daughter, Libby, woke up this morning with the pink eye, so she brought her to work with her."

"I got here early," the mother, Mrs. Palmer, spoke up, "and took Libby inside the gift shop with me. I told her to stay in the play area while I grabbed something from the car, and when I returned, the back door was open and Libby was gone. I never heard or saw anything to make me think that someone might...might have taken her."

Mrs. Palmer broke down and started to cry then, and Zaylie's heart went out to her.

"We've searched the area as best we can," Bill said, "but the fog is so thick, it's hard to see much of anything."

"Do you have something of your daughter's that my dog can get a scent from?" Zaylie asked Mrs. Palmer.

The woman hurried to her car and brought back a stuffed animal. "Please find my baby," she whispered brokenly. "She's only six, and so little."

Zaylie took the toy and squeezed the woman's hand. "I'll do my best," she promised.

Telling Mrs. Palmer to stay inside the gift shop with the only other police officer around, Bill led Zaylie and Ryker out the back door.

"I know it's still early, but the fort will remain closed while we search the place," he told her. "I have my other men stationed around the perimeter just in case anyone suspicious tries to sneak out of here."

The ground was soft and the air was covered in

a thick, white cloud when they stepped outside. Zaylie allowed Smutti to sniff Libby's little toy, and then she gave the signal to start searching. Smutti's nose immediately went to the ground and she circled the area for a few seconds before finding a definite scent.

"Let's hope she's close by," Zaylie muttered as they all followed Smutti, who slid quietly through the mist like a black shadow.

As they walked further, ruins of the old fort began rising up around them like jagged silhouettes from the past. In the thick fog, Zaylie could almost see the gray shadows of Confederate soldiers ducking behind the brick walls and stone barricades. Smutti led them to an uneven set of stairs, and as they carefully ascended the stone walkway, a cracked, black cannon came into view.

The area was still and quiet. The only sound that could be heard was the crunching of their footsteps and the peaceful trickle of the river that ran close by. When they reached the top of the wall, Smutti drew very close to the edge as she tracked the scent. Zaylie's heart caught. Had Libby climbed to the top and fallen over the edge? They all stopped and peered down, but the fog was too thick. They couldn't see the ground.

Just then, Smutti turned and headed to the other end of the wall, where another set of stairs awaited them. They climbed back down to the courtyard, and Zaylie was surprised when Smutti picked up her pace and turned toward the woods that rested several yards behind the fort. As they headed that way, Bill's walkie-talkie buzzed.

"Sheriff, there's a suspicious-looking man over here on the south end," one of the officers said. "You'd better come check it out."

"Go ahead," Zaylie told him. "We'll keep looking. Call me if you find her."

As Bill hurried away, his figure quickly melting into the fog, Smutti led Zaylie and Ryker into the woods. The small path wound through the oak-shaded forest, with silvery moss hanging from the branches that towered overhead. The area was eerily quiet. There were no birds chirping in the trees or squirrels rustling among the bushes, and with the thick moisture that hung in the air, Zaylie suddenly felt chilled.

"There's an earthwork around here somewhere," Ryker stated, his deep voice rumbling in the silence.

"There," Zaylie replied, pointing to what appeared to be an opening in the forest a few steps ahead.

The trees parted, and the stone pathway turned into grass. The sound of the river grew louder the further they walked, and through the fog, a large mound of earth formed up ahead.

"Do you think she came all the way out here?" Ryker asked in a low tone.

Before Zaylie could reply, Smutti suddenly stopped and lifted her head, her ears twitching.

"She hears something," Zaylie whispered.

Leaning over, she rubbed Smutti's back and asked, "What is it, girl?"

Without making a sound, Smutti began moving forward again. It appeared she was leading them straight into the heart of the mound, and even through the fog, Zaylie could see how dark it was inside.

"Smutti, wait," Zaylie commanded, and the dog stopped while her master pulled a flashlight from her pocket. Handing it to Ryker, she said, "Shine this inside as we enter. And just in case we need it, I hope you remember all of your combat training."

"Don't worry," he replied as he clicked on the light. "I've got you covered."

The three slowly moved forward, and as the beam from the flashlight bounced along the dark brown earthen walls, it finally landed on a small, trembling figure crouched in the corner.

CHAPTER 12

L ibby?"
Zaylie's voice echoed in the small room, and she had to hold tightly to Smutti's leash as the dog strained to get closer to the little girl. Frightened eyes reflected in the light, and Zaylie quickly looked around the room in search of a more dangerous subject.

"Honey, are you alright?" Zaylie asked as she slowly walked closer to the child.

"I-I want my mommy," the little girl sniffled.

Zaylie allowed Smutti to approach the girl first, and she watched Libby's fear melt away as the dog gently nudged the child with her nose. With a sob, Libby threw her arms around Smutti's neck and buried her face in the dog's fur.

Zaylie kneeled beside her and said softly, "My name is Zaylie, and this is Smutti. She's my search and rescue dog. Would you like to hold her leash as she leads us back to your mommy?"

With a sniff, Libby nodded, and Zaylie helped the little girl up. As they left the dark hole in the earth and headed back toward the gift shop, Zaylie called Bill to give him the good news. Not every mission was successful, but she was thankful this one was. She didn't know what had happened yet, but Libby had been safely found, and she said a prayer of thanks under her breath.

When they all got back to the gift shop, Mrs. Palmer rushed to her daughter's side and pulled her into her arms.

"Baby, what happened?" she asked as tears dripped down her face.

"I saw a rabbit out the window and went outside to play with it," Libby told her mom. "B-but then I got lost in the fog, and I thought somebody was chasing me. Oh, Mama, I was so scared!"

"Did you find anyone?" Zaylie asked Bill in a low voice.

"A homeless man," he replied. "He was still drunk from the night before, so he could have been who Libby heard."

"Or it might have just been her imagination," Ryker spoke up. "She was lost and scared and may have just thought she heard someone."

Bill agreed, and after Libby and her mom thanked Zaylie for her help, she said her goodbyes and left.

As they walked back to Ryker's truck, he nudged Zaylie with his elbow. "You and I make a pretty good team, don't we?" he asked, wiggling his eyebrows.

"Don't you mean Smutti and I make a good team?" she replied. Looking over at him, she added with a smirk, "I seem to remember you just followed along the whole time."

"Hey, I held the flashlight," he stated, opening the passenger side door for Zaylie. "And my ninja skills were always there, ready and waiting in case you needed them."

"Maybe one day you'll get a chance to use them," she replied teasingly.

"Keep being mean to me, and I just might," he shot back with a wink.

Once they were back on the road, Zaylie asked, "Is this fog ever going to lift?"

"It's supposed to clear up by ten o'clock, but..." Ryker hesitated. "Wait, what's that?"

Looking ahead to where Ryker's gaze was directed, Zaylie could see flashing yellow lights emerging from the fog.

"Looks like someone had an accident," she commented as Ryker pulled over behind the truck and trailer and climbed out.

"Is everything alright?" Ryker asked, cautiously approaching the driver's side door.

The door swung open, and Clark Schultz stepped out. "I hit a deer," he stated in a gruff voice. "I'm waiting on a tow truck to get here."

"Could we drive you somewhere?" Zaylie asked as she walked toward the two men.

Clark glanced at her in surprise, and then his tight, annoyed expression relaxed into a smile. "That's very nice of you to offer, Miss Layne, but the tow should be here any minute."

Zaylie surveyed the damage to his front right fender and shook her head. "I'm sorry this happened, but it's difficult to see a deer in this fog."

Clark nodded. "Yeah, plus I'm worn out from a

long haul. I drove all night to get home."

"Where did you drive from?" Ryker asked.

Clark hesitated, but before he could answer, the sound of an approaching large truck interrupted the conversation.

"Well, here's that tow," he stated. Stepping around Ryker, Clark reached for Zaylie's hand and said, "It was nice to see you again, Miss Layne. Y'all be careful, okay?"

As they drove away, Ryker asked, "How do you know Clark so well?"

"I actually don't know him that well at all," she replied. "Do you?"

Ryker shook his head. "No," he said as he turned down her driveway. "He's made some deliveries for my dad in the past, but he's not the overly friendly type." Glancing over at Zaylie with a smirk, he added, "Unless he's around you, that is."

Zaylie chuckled. "Maybe it's Smutti he likes. When someone isn't a people person, they usually like animals. Actually," she added with a laugh, "I'm sort of that way, too."

Ryker raised his eyebrows and looked at her in surprise as he pulled up in front of the house and parked. "Why don't you like people?" he wanted to know.

Zaylie opened the truck door and started to climb out. "I like *some* people," she replied, letting Smutti out the back. "But animals won't hurt you like people can. I trust Smutti more than most humans."

"Am I part of the group of people you like?" he wanted to know.

Patting him on the arm, Zaylie said, "Don't ask," and then walked into the house before he could reply.

Later that afternoon, Zaylie was pouring over Zoe's case files when her phone alerted her to an incoming email. Ignoring it, Zaylie pushed her phone aside and continued to study the police report after Zoe's body was found. She had to force her emotions to remain neutral as she read, as if the report was about a complete stranger instead of her sister.

"At 7:03 a.m. on the morning of June the 25th, the body of a young woman was found in the park by a jogger (his name and address are listed below). The body was identified by Arnold Layne as his oldest daughter, Zoe Layne. She was fifteen years old, 5'4" tall, with red hair and hazel eyes. The coroner will do an official autopsy, but it appears she was either strangled or smothered. The area has been thoroughly investigated, but no evidence can be found. It is apparent that her body was out in the elements for several days before being found."

The report was handwritten, and Zaylie recognized Uncle Bill's bold, slanted penmanship. She knew how hard this had been on him, and she could almost see the struggle behind each word that was written.

There were photographs of Zoe's body, but Zaylie had never been able to force herself to look at them. A few years ago, she'd spoken to the jogger, Hal Bronson, who was now in his fifties. He'd told her exactly what he'd told the police, which was that he saw what appeared to be an arm protruding from beneath some leaves and moss near the path where he was jogging, and he'd immediately phoned the police. Zaylie had wondered for a while if he was somehow involved in Zoe's kidnapping and death, but both he and his wife confirmed that they'd been out of town on vacation until the day before the body was found.

Setting the police report aside, Zaylie picked up a plastic bag that held the clothes Zoe had been wearing and her charm bracelet. Pulling the bracelet out, Zaylie remembered overhearing Uncle Bill asking her parents if they wanted the bracelet and her clothes back after the case was closed.

"Burn everything," her mother had said, and Zaylie remembered thinking how strange it was that someone's voice could sound so hard and broken all at once.

"Just leave it all in her case box," her father told Bill with a sigh. *"Who knows, the investigation may be re-opened someday."*

Zaylie's eyes filled with tears at the painful memory, and she was just about to put the bracelet back into the bag when something suddenly caught her attention. Holding the piece of jewelry up to the light, Zaylie realized one of the charms was missing. The bracelet had so many that it was hard to notice, but Zaylie remembered that specific charm because Zoe showed it to her a few nights before she was kidnapped.

"Don't tell Mom and Dad or Erica," she'd said. *"This one will be our little secret."*

With wide eyes, Zaylie stared at the tiny silver heart and asked, *"Why don't you want anyone else to know about it?"*

Smiling softly, Zoe explained, *"Because someone special gave it to me, and I don't want anyone to know about it yet."*

Sitting back against the chair, Zaylie shook her head in disbelief. How had she completely forgotten about that? Rubbing her temples, she closed her eyes and tried to remember more. She was almost positive there had been initials engraved on the heart, but for the life of her, she couldn't remember what they were. Why was the heart missing, though? And when had it been taken? Zaylie thought she remembered that Zoe was wearing it when they were drawing together the night she was taken. She couldn't be certain, though. Since she hadn't even remembered its existence until now, she couldn't be certain of anything.

With a sigh, she placed the bracelet back into the box and picked up her phone. The new email blinked across the screen, and she tapped on it, not recognizing the sender. When a large image filled the body of the email, Zaylie felt the blood leave her face. The image was of a bloodied and bruised young woman, and she was tied to a tree. Her eyes were open and frightened, tear-filled eyes stared back at the camera. Typed below the image were these words:

WANT TO PLAY GAMES WITH ME? FINE. CAN YOU FIND HER BEFORE IT'S TOO LATE?

CHAPTER 13

After receiving the email, Zaylie immediately called Bill.

"Forward the email to me and then come to the station," he told her.

Zaylie was at the police department within fifteen minutes. When she hurried into Bill's office, Devon was there with him.

"I've contacted a friend at the FBI," Bill said when he saw her. "He's checking to see if anyone matching this young woman's description has been reported missing in the state of Georgia in the last few days."

"What if she's not in Georgia?" Zaylie wanted to know.

Bill rubbed the back of his neck. "If she's not in Georgia, I doubt we'll ever find her. He's also trying to trace the IP address, but that could turn out to be a dead end and cause us to waste valuable time that we don't have."

"Why?" Zaylie wanted to know.

"Because the killer could have easily gone to another city or state and sent that email."

Zaylie sighed. "Even if we do figure out where she lives, how are we going to find her?" she asked. "There isn't much to go on in that picture."

"I was actually able to clean it up a bit,"

Devon stated, beckoning for Zaylie to look at Bill's computer screen. When she moved to stand behind them both, he pointed to the picture and asked, "See that break in the trees there behind her left shoulder? It looks like a body of water. So, if we can figure out who she is, maybe the police can narrow down the general area by searching near lakes and rivers."

"That's a good start," she said with a nod. Patting Devon on the shoulder, she added, "Good work, Devon. It's a good thing you were here."

"Thanks," Devon replied. "Uncle Bill, while you wait for your contact to call, could I be of any more help?"

"I've got a few men searching for news articles and alerts in Georgia for missing women," Bill stated.

"Devon and I can search social media for the same thing," Zaylie said.

Thirty minutes passed, and all of their efforts were coming up empty. Zaylie was just about to wonder if they'd be able to find any leads at all when Bill's phone rang.

"It's my friend with the FBI," he said as he quickly answered the call and put it on speakerphone. "Hey, Ed, tell me you've got something?"

"A young woman matching the description of the girl in the photo went missing yesterday morning," Ed replied. "Her name is Tia Anders, and she's from Alpharetta. It appears the email was sent from a burner phone using public Wi-fi from a café in Atlanta. I'm sending a unit out to Alpharetta now; they should be there within a couple of hours."

"I'm coming, too," Zaylie spoke up.

"Ed, would it be okay if I meet your unit up there?" Bill asked. "I may bring a couple of people with me to help with the search."

"Normally, I would say it's not necessary," Ed replied. "But a bad storm is supposed to hit the Alpharetta area tomorrow afternoon, so we need all the help we can get or we may lose the trail."

"We'll be there as soon as we can," Bill promised, and the call was ended. Grabbing his car keys, Bill said to Devon, "I'm going home to grab a few things. Would you have time to get airline tickets for Zaylie and me?" When Devon nodded, Bill added, "If there are no flights available in the next two hours, let me know and we'll just drive. Zaylie, go home and grab whatever you need and meet me back here."

Zaylie nodded, and as she hurried out to her car, her fingers shook as she opened the car door. What if they couldn't find Tia in time? An internal clock was ticking, and Zaylie could hear it pounding loudly inside her head with each passing second.

Thankfully, Devon was able to snag a flight leaving Savannah within the hour. Zaylie, Smutti, and Bill rushed to the airport, and after going through security, they had to run through the terminal to keep from missing their flight. By the time they were on the plane and in their seats, they were all out of breath. Zaylie was still sore from the attack, and her lower back ached from the exertion.

They arrived in Atlanta in less than two hours and picked up the rental car Devon had reserved for them. It was normally a thirty minute drive to Alpharetta, but with the late afternoon traffic in the city, it took nearly two hours to reach the small town. By the time they arrived at the local police station, everyone was there going over the plan for the next morning.

"I'm Agent Ellington. Ed Hallows told me you'd be coming," the lead FBI agent said to Bill as the two shook hands. When Bill introduced him to Zaylie, Ellington said, "I'm sorry, but civilians aren't allowed on this search." Looking down at Smutti, he added, "We also have our own dogs."

"Miss Layne is who the kidnapper initially contacted," Bill explained. "She's been tracking this man for years; we believe he kidnapped and killed her sister."

Ellington wasn't budging. "It's too dangerous," he stated firmly. "And we don't need anyone who isn't properly trained possibly botching this search."

"My dog and I are both SAR certified," Zaylie spoke up, showing him her credentials.

"She owns the Crescent Moon K-9 Training

Center in Tennessee," Bill told him. "I'm sure you've heard of their impeccable reputation. They have contracts with several law enforcement agencies throughout the country."

After studying the credentials, Ellington looked up at Zaylie and asked, "Your dog is trained in both scent specific tracking *and* air scent?"

By the way he voiced the question, Zaylie knew he was dubious. Having such a dog was rare, and she was used to the skepticism.

Zaylie nodded. "Yes, sir."

Ellington's eyes narrowed. "That's almost unheard of, Miss Layne," he stated. "Even if a dog is cross-trained to do tracking *and* air scent, it's very rare for a dog to be scent specific in both areas."

Holding his gaze, Zaylie replied smoothly, "Let us join the search tomorrow and prove that even though it is rare, it's not impossible."

Ellington studied her for a moment, his eyes narrowed.

"We need all the help we can get," the local sheriff spoke up. His last name was Irving, and he appeared to be in his late forties.

After a moment, Ellington sighed and said, "Fine. But if you or your dog interfere in any way, you're out."

Zaylie agreed, and they moved on to discuss the case. She was relieved that Ellington was allowing them to join the search. She felt it was her fault that Tia had been taken, and being part of the search was important to her for more reasons than one.

Reaching for a photograph that lay on his desk, Sheriff Irving held it up for Zaylie and Bill to see. "Here is a recent picture of Tia," he told them. "Her parents brought it in this morning when they notified us that she was missing."

"Where was she last seen?" Zaylie wanted to know, studying the picture closely.

Moving to stand next to a map hanging nearby, Ellington pointed to a location near the river and said, "Her best friend told us they would meet to go jogging every morning at a nearby park, but Tia texted her at the last minute and canceled. We traced her phone and found it here, along with her car, at the Chattahoochee River Recreation Area."

"Did you check for fingerprints?" Bill asked.

Ellington nodded. "The only prints we found were hers," he replied. "We also went by her apartment, but there was no evidence of foul play."

Zaylie stood before the map, her mind whirling. Had Tia simply been in the wrong place at the wrong time, or had the kidnapper been stalking her for several weeks? If that were the case, though, why had he taken Lauren? Perhaps Lauren had been the main target, but when Zaylie interrupted his plan, he took Tia as a way to punish Zaylie. But why Tia? She and Lauren were both in their early twenties, but that's where the resemblance ended. Lauren's features were similar to Zoe's; fair and pixie-like, with hazel eyes and reddish blonde hair. Tia, on the other hand, was tall and slim, with dark hair and dark eyes.

What am I missing? she wondered. It seemed strange that Tia changed her jogging date at the last minute. Had she simply decided she wanted to do something different and drove out to the river for a few moments of peace when she stumbled upon the kidnapper? Or perhaps it was something else altogether.

"Does Tia have a boyfriend?" Zaylie asked, turning to face everyone.

"Her parents said no, but her best friend said she thought there was someone Tia was seeing," Sheriff Irving replied. "She doesn't know who he is, though. Every time she would ask Tia about it, she'd deny it."

"Well, we'll be here in the morning to help with the search," Bill said after they'd talked a bit longer. "Is there anywhere to stay nearby?"

"There's a nice hotel just down the road," the sheriff said, pointing to the left of the station entrance. "See y'all in the morning."

As they drove away from the station, Bill glanced over at Zaylie and said, "When we join the search tomorrow, I want you to stick by my side, okay? This guy targeted you, Zaylie. He's angry that you interfered with Lauren, and he's out to get you. I probably shouldn't have even let you come."

Zaylie patted him on the arm reassuringly and said, "I'll be careful, Uncle Bill. I promise. Plus, you'll be watching my back, so there's no need to worry."

Silence filled the car then, and Zaylie glanced out the window into the darkness of the night. She knew Bill was right; this guy was after her, but she couldn't sit by and do nothing while a helpless young woman suffered because of her.

Glancing back at Smutti, she thought, *We'll find her. We've got to.*

CHAPTER 14

At seven o'clock the next morning, Zaylie and Bill drove out to the Chattahoochee to meet up with the search party. When they arrived at the area sectioned off by the FBI, Zaylie was surprised to see a familiar face among the group standing at the command post.

"Bill, what is Ryker doing here?" she asked, her brow furrowing as she climbed from the rental car.

Bill shrugged. "No idea," he replied.

Ryker waved to them and stepped away from the other agents when they drew closer.

"Your grandmother asked me to come," he told Zaylie, holding up his hands when she opened her mouth to question him. "She's worried about you and it didn't take her long to talk me into coming up here to help out with the search."

"To keep an eye on me, you mean," Zaylie stated dryly, crossing her arms

"I guess she doesn't trust *me* to do that," Bill said in a slightly offended tone.

"I think her idea was the more the merrier," Ryker said, chuckling as he clapped Bill on the shoulder.

"Good morning," Agent Ellington said as he joined their group. "I see you've all met. Is everyone ready to get started?"

Zaylie glanced at Ryker and frowned. "You mean you're letting him join the search?" she asked Ellington.

He nodded. "Of course I am. He's a SEAL," he said, as if that explained everything.

As he turned and walked away, Zaylie crossed her arms and asked sarcastically, "So, if I'd told him last night that I was a SEAL, I guess he wouldn't have been so hesitant to let me join the search?"

Ryker laughed, and Bill said, "Let it go, Zaylie. He agreed to let you join, didn't he?"

"He wasn't happy about it, though," she replied in an annoyed tone.

Shaking his head, Bill walked ahead to join the others. With a grin, Ryker said, "I guess everyone can't be special like me."

Glancing sideways at him, Zaylie smirked and said glibly, "Aren't we all thankful for that."

"Everyone, listen up!"

Ellington's announcement meant that the search was about to be underway, and everyone quickly gathered in to listen to his instructions.

"The dogs and their handlers will go out front, so there won't be any cross-contamination," he said, glancing over at the two agents who stood off to the side with their German Shepherds. "The rest of us will follow behind. The dogs will be doing what we call a hasty search, so I want the rest of you to spread out and carefully search the ground as you go. We're in a crunch for time, I know, but I don't want us to overlook anything, if at all possible. The area has been evacuated and sealed off, so you shouldn't see any hikers or tourists."

"Will you and Smutti also be going ahead?" Ryker asked Zaylie, keeping his voice low.

"I doubt it," she said with a sigh. "He'll probably expect us to stay behind. Even so, Smutti will still be able to track Tia's scent."

"I'm giving you all a pre-programmed walkie-talkie," Ellington continued, nodding to one of the other agents who was ready to hand out the devices. "Let me know the moment you find anything. This man could be very dangerous, so I want all of you to be on guard at all times. Any questions?"

When no one spoke up, he nodded and said, "Alright, let's get going. Tia's parents gave me one of her sweaters; I have it here in a bag for the dogs to use for a scent."

As Zaylie led Smutti forward to take her turn sniffing the sweater, she asked Ellington if they could work ahead with the other dogs.

"No, stay back with the others," he replied. When she started to protest, he held up his hand and snapped, "Don't push me, Miss Layne. If your dog is as good as you say, maybe she'll find something our dogs miss."

Zaylie sighed with frustration but didn't attempt to protest further. She and Smutti stepped back and watched as the dogs smelled the sweater and then immediately set out searching for a scent. In just a matter of seconds, they'd found one and were leading their handlers into the woods, with Ellington and Sheriff Irving hurrying after them.

"He wouldn't let you go, huh?" Ryker asked as he stepped up next to Zaylie.

She shook her head. "No," she replied. Suddenly, it hit her what Ellington had said earlier, and she looked up at Ryker and asked with wide eyes, "Wait, you were a SEAL?"

Ryker chuckled. "Takes you a little while to process things sometimes, doesn't it? Yes, I was a SEAL."

Zaylie was floored. She'd known Ryker was in the Navy, but she'd had no idea he was part of such an elite unit.

"Wow, I'm impressed," she told him.

"Maybe now you'll learn to appreciate me more," he replied with a wink.

"Don't push your luck," she retorted with a smile.

Now that the dogs were a proper distance ahead, Zaylie grabbed the bag with Tia's sweater that Ellington had left behind and they joined the other agents in the ground search. The dogs had left the hiking trail almost immediately, so Zaylie and the others followed their general path through the thick woods. The going was slow and tedious as they kept their eyes trained on the ground. Leaves and fallen branches were scattered along the forest floor, and Smutti's ears perked up at the sound of a squirrel rustling in the bushes to their left.

"Look at this," Ryker said, kneeling to point at a partially hidden footprint.

"Do you think it's our guy's?" Bill asked him.

"Judging by the way it's half-hidden by leaves, I'd say it's a possibility," he replied.

"I'll measure the print and mark the area," one of the agents told them when he saw what they'd found. "Call it into Ellington, will you?"

Bill said he would, and as they continued on their way, he radioed the news in to Ellington.

"Good find," Zaylie told Ryker.

"It's not the first shoe print I've ever found," he replied with a slight smile.

"I guess you're almost as good of a tracker as Smutti," she stated teasingly.

Ryker grinned. "Nah, I could never come close to being that good," he said, reaching down to rub Smutti's ears.

The further they went, the more tense and anxious Zaylie felt. It was still early in the day, but the wind was picking up and she could feel the storm drawing closer. The sky was already darkening, and thick clouds covered the sun, making it harder for their group to search the ground for clues. Would they find anything before the storm hit? That question continually ran through everyone's mind. Even though the dogs could still detect scent in the rain, it was dangerous to continue a search during a storm. And a heavy rain could potentially wash away the majority of the scent.

The backpack Zaylie always carried seemed to weigh her down more than normal. What if they didn't find Tia in time? What if they never caught this man, and he continued to kill innocent women? The thought of her sister's killer never coming to justice broke Zaylie's heart.

Nearly two hours had passed when Ellington's voice crackled over the radio, and they all stopped to listen.

"We're near the river," he said. "The dogs found the spot where the photograph was taken, but Tia isn't here."

"Can you keep tracking her from there?" Bill wanted to know.

"No. The dogs lost the trail."

Zaylie, Smutti, Ryker, and Bill left the search group and hurried ahead to join Ellington and his team.

"Wow," Zaylie breathed once they reached the area that was currently being roped off.

Carved into the large oak where Tia had been tied up to take the picture was the word "Gotcha". Apparently, the kidnapper was toying with them. The river could be seen through the trees just up ahead, and Zaylie felt a chill wash over her. The killer had been here, in this very location, only hours before. The question was, though, where did he go from here?

"Your dogs can't track from here?" Ryker asked Ellington.

The agent ran a hand over his bald head and

sighed. "They keep getting confused," he replied, his voice heavy with frustration. "My guess is that the kidnapper carried Tia away from here, and by the dogs' behavior, he did a lot of circling and backtracking to throw us off."

"Would it be okay if Smutti tried?" Zaylie asked him.

When Ellington nodded, Zaylie pulled the bag with Tia's sweater from her backpack and held it out for Smutti to smell. Her dog sniffed the sweater, and when Zaylie gave the command, she began searching. They all stood quietly by, watching as Smutti searched the ground first. She immediately picked up on a scent, but just like the other dogs, she lost it just as quickly. Zaylie held her breath, watching at Smutti lifted her nose and began to sniff the air. She moved around for a moment, taking in the wind currents, and suddenly her ears perked up and she let out a sharp bark.

"She's got a scent," Zaylie cried.

Ellington's eyes widened in surprise as Smutti took off through the forest, and everyone leaped into action. Ellington shouted a few commands to the agents at the scene, and then quickly hurried after Zaylie and the others.

Smutti led them through a maze of trees and bushes, and over downed limbs and logs. The sound of the river could be heard coming from their left, but all Zaylie listened for was the jingling of the bell on Smutti's collar. She didn't expect

Smutti to lead them directly to the kidnapper; he was too smart for that. But she hoped to find Tia, and she hoped to find her alive.

Suddenly, the sound of the bell stopped. They all stopped running and listened, their hearts all pounding in unison. Ellington, Bill, and Sheriff Irving pulled their guns from their holsters, and Zaylie searched the trees, looking for Smutti's familiar black shadow. Where was she? Why wasn't she barking or returning to Zaylie? Had something happened?

Just as Zaylie opened her mouth to whistle for her dog, Smutti barked loudly. With a breath of relief, Zaylie said, "Come on. She's found something."

They all hurried forward, stopping when they reached an opening and a small dirt road. Smutti sat on one side, staring down the road with her nose twitching in the air. She turned to look at her master, and Zaylie's heart dropped.

"She's lost the scent," she stated in a heavy voice.

CHAPTER 15

The kidnapper must have had a car parked back here and left with Tia in it," Zaylie said as she went over to rub Smutti on the head.

"There are a few tire tracks over here," Ryker pointed out.

"Most of them probably belong to the park rangers that patrol the area," Irving replied. "It looks like we've hit a dead end."

"Where does this road lead?" Ellington asked. "Would there be security cameras anywhere along the way?"

Irving shook his head. "No, I'm afraid not."

"So, what now?" Zaylie asked, feeling rather discouraged.

"It looks like we're back to square one," Ellington replied with a sigh. "I'll have one of my men go out to that café in Atlanta to check the cameras, but I doubt anything will come of it. This guy is too smart to let his face be caught on camera."

They all walked back to the place in the woods where the photograph had been taken, and Zaylie felt a fierce sense of frustration. Why did he send her that picture? Why did he want her to come here? Was he simply toying with her?

"We should go," Bill told Zaylie. "Ellington said he'll let us know if they find anything."

Zaylie nodded, and after waving goodbye to Ellington, they made their trek back through the woods. As they walked, Zaylie noticed that Smutti's tail was down and her ears weren't as perky as normal. It seemed that she felt as despondent as Zaylie at not finding Tia, but such an emotion was common in SAR dogs. During the search for survivors after the World Trade Center disaster, many of the dogs became depressed. With the overwhelming smell of death and the fact that very few survivors were found, it was just too much to cope with, and some never worked as SAR dogs again.

By the time they made it back to their vehicles, it was just past noon. Ryker suggested they go get something to eat, but Bill said he was tired and wanted to go back to the hotel to lie down.

"You kids go ahead," he told them.

"Would you take Smutti back with you?" Zaylie asked him. "It's been a long morning for her, and I think she needs some rest."

Bill agreed, and after the two had left, Zaylie climbed into Ryker's truck. As they drove away, she stared out the window at the police cars, and with a heavy heart, she wondered if they'd ever find Tia.

"Hey, why don't we drive into Atlanta and surprise Rita?" Ryker asked.

With a smile spreading across her face, Zaylie turned to smile at him and said, "That's a great idea. Should we call and find out where she is?"

"Nah, I have one of those family tracker apps on

my phone," he said, pulling his cell phone out of his pocket. "Here, take this and let me know where she is."

"Was this tracker app her idea or yours?" Zaylie asked as she opened the app.

"Definitely mine," he replied with a chuckle.

"It looks like she's at the theater," Zaylie said. "I guess they're doing rehearsals. Do you think they'll let us in?"

"What a silly question to ask an ex-SEAL," Ryker replied with a twinkle in his eyes.

An hour later, Zaylie and Ryker sneaked quietly into the back of the theater. The sound of music and laughter could be heard reverberating throughout the massive building, and Zaylie gasped when she caught her foot on a fallen prop.

"You're going to get us shot," she whispered, grabbing Ryker's arm to keep from falling.

"Theater people don't carry guns," he stated. "Besides, don't you trust me to protect you?"

"Can I get back to you on that one?"

"You hurt me, Miss Layne," Ryker said with a dramatic sigh.

As they rounded a dark corner and opened a door, they stopped to stare at what could only be the backstage. Costumes lay scattered about, lights overhead flicked on and off to the beat of the music, and actors and dancers scurried about like ants. The energy in the air was palpable, and Zaylie had to pause to catch her breath.

"Uh, can I help you?"

They both turned to find a man in his mid-fifties, wearing a bowtie and a quizzical expression.

"We're looking for Rita Steele," Ryker said, stepping forward to shake the man's hand. "I'm her brother, Ryker, and this is her best friend, Zaylie Layne."

The man's eyes widened, and he smiled. "Ah, yes, I've heard Rita speak of you both quite often. She's out on stage at the moment, but she'll be coming back here shortly."

The man led them to stage left, where they stood on the sidelines and watched. Rita played her part beautifully, as usual, but Zaylie thought her friend seemed a bit distracted. The usual sparkle in her eyes wasn't quite as bright as it normally was, and when one of the directors touched her arm and whispered something to her, she jerked away.

"What do you think that was about?" Zaylie asked Ryker.

Before Ryker could answer, Rita's part was finished, and she was heading their way. When she saw them, her eyes flew open wide and she screamed like a banshee as she raced toward them. Ryker stepped forward and caught his sister as she leaped into his arms, and after twirling her around, he set her down to give Zaylie a turn.

"What are y'all doing here?" Rita squealed with excitement as she pulled Zaylie into a crushing hug.

"We'll have to explain all that later," Zaylie said, pulling back to smile at her gorgeous friend, "but we wanted to surprise you. Can you go to lunch with us?"

Rita nodded exuberantly, her black hair shining in the overhead lights. "Give me five minutes to change, and I'll..."

"Rita, you were amazing!"

They all turned to find a man hurrying up the stage stairs toward Rita. When he held his face up to the light, Zaylie blinked.

"Kaleb?" she asked in surprise.

Kaleb Bates faltered a bit in his steps when he recognized Rita's friend as she stepped forward from the shadows. Raising his eyebrows, he looked between the three of them with a bit of uncertainty.

"Y'all know each other?" Rita asked, beckoning for Kaleb to join them.

"Yes, we met in West Virginia last week," Zaylie replied. "Kaleb helped save my life."

"What a small world!" Rita exclaimed as she looped a hand through his arm. "Kaleb and I met last month when he was here on business. He came to the show and stayed around afterward to meet me." Glancing up at her clearly uncomfortable companion, she batted her eyes and added, "I guess my dazzling performance just swept him off his feet."

"Oh, it definitely did," he replied, smiling down

at Rita.

"Is anyone going to introduce me?" Ryker cleared his throat, his tone a little testy.

"Oh! I'm sorry, Ryker, I forgot you were standing there." Rita giggled. "Kaleb Bates, meet my handsome twin brother, Ryker."

The two men shook hands, both standing a little taller as they sized each other up. Zaylie studied Kaleb, thinking how strange it was to see him here with her best friend. Rita thought it was coincidental, but Zaylie had always been the suspicious type. What Kaleb could be up to, though, she had no idea. Perhaps it really was just a coincidence like Rita said.

"Well, I'm going to go change my clothes and then the four of us can go out to eat."

As Rita hurried off toward her dressing room, Zaylie watched as Ryker pursed his lips in irritation. They hadn't expected to have to share Rita's company with a fourth party, and both were a bit put out about it.

As Kaleb went outside to pull his car around, Zaylie looked at Ryker and shrugged. "I guess this is what happens when you surprise someone," she said.

"Well, I know one thing. I intend to check this Bates guy out," Ryker stated. "How exactly did he help save your life, anyway?"

"Okay, I'm ready!" Rita called as she all but hopped across the backstage toward Zaylie and her brother. Taking Zaylie's hand, she pulled her toward the back door and said, "Now, tell me exactly how Kaleb saved your life. I want every little juicy detail."

All during lunch, Zaylie kept checking her phone to see if Bill had sent any updates about Tia. So far, the only texts she'd received were from Gran, and she could barely decipher them.

"Either put your glasses on or do voice texting," Zaylie sent Gran with a laughing emoji. *"You know your texts are basically unreadable otherwise."*

In a moment, Gran replied, *"Sorry! How are you, honey? Are you making sure to stay with Ryker or Bill at all times?"*

Zaylie shook her head. *"Yes, ma'am,"* she replied like a dutiful granddaughter. *"I'll be careful. Don't worry about me."*

"Any word from Bill?" Ryker asked Zaylie.

Putting her phone back into her purse, Zaylie said, "No, unfortunately not."

"It's scary to think that this guy is so close by," Rita stated with a shiver.

"You really think it's the same man who killed Lauren?" Kaleb asked, taking a sip of his sweet tea.

Zaylie nodded. "I do," she replied. "Hey, do you know if the police found any fingerprints on that note Lauren left? I asked them to let me know, but I haven't heard from them."

"I bumped into Officer Turner before I left," he replied, "and he said there was one other print besides Lauren's, but it was too smudged to use."

Zaylie sighed. "I guess they're still busy trying to find that arsonist." Eyeing Kaleb, she asked, "So, are you going to be visiting Rita often?"

Kaleb smiled at Rita and said, "It's possible."

With a grin, Rita leaned closer to him and said flirtatiously, "You'd better."

Kaleb reached out and draped his arm around Rita's shoulders. "Oh, yeah?" he asked warmly.

"How are your brothers, Kaleb?" Zaylie asked, trying to change the subject before Ryker's face got any redder. "You said you have two, right?"

Shifting in his seat, Kaleb moved his arm and stammered, "Uh, well, no. I have three brothers."

Zaylie raised her eyebrows in mock surprise. "Oh? I could have sworn you told me two."

"Barley is my younger brother," Kaleb replied, his eyes trained on the nearly empty plate of food before him. "He still lives back home."

"My goodness, I can't imagine having *three* brothers," Rita stated with a sigh.

"Is that the man I saw you talking to on the street after we got back from searching the cabin?"

Kaleb looked up at Zaylie in surprise, but it seemed she could also see a hint of anger in his eyes.

"Yes, it was," he all but ground out.

Before Zaylie could tell him about seeing Barley at her hotel that night, he glanced at his watch and announced that he had to leave.

"So soon?" Rita asked with a frown.

"Yeah, sorry. I have an appointment in the next twenty minutes, and I didn't realize how late it had gotten," he replied. Throwing a chunk of cash onto the table, he stood and said, "That should cover our bill. Ryker, it was nice meeting you. Rita, I'll call you tonight, okay? See y'all later."

They all sat in silence as they watched Kaleb hurry from the restaurant. Did he really have an appointment, or was the conversation somehow making him uncomfortable?

Stop being so suspicious, she scolded herself. *Kaleb is a nice guy. He even helped save your life, for Pete's sake!*

Zaylie's phone chimed, and she glanced at the screen, hoping the text was from Bill. She sighed with frustration when she saw Gran's name flash across the screen once again. Would they ever find Tia? Was it hopeless to wish for a happy ending?

The conversation between Rita and Ryker soon caught Zaylie's attention, and she forced herself to join the discussion about "the good ole days". She didn't know when she'd get to see her best friend again, and she wanted to enjoy the time she had to spend with her. The thought of Tia and her sister's killer, though, always lingered in the back of her mind.

CHAPTER 16

L ater that night, Zaylie listened to the rain as it beat against the hotel window when her phone suddenly alerted her to an incoming email. She unlocked the screen, her eyes widening at the subject line: **Open, or Tia dies.**

Hurriedly, Zaylie opened the email and watched as a photo of Tia loaded onto her screen. The young woman was bound and gagged, and it appeared she was inside a dilapidated old building. Scrolling down, Zaylie read the message: *Come alone, no cops & no dog, & I'll trade Tia for you. I'll even tell you about your sister. If you disobey me, I'll kill her.*

Zaylie felt her blood run cold. Her eyes scanned over the address listed beneath the message, and she pondered what to do. If she went, she'd be giving her own life for Tia's. Would he really let Tia go, though, or would he simply kill them both? If she took her gun, perhaps she could find a way to save both Tia *and* herself. It was a risk, but she had to take it.

With quick, jerky movements, she slid into a raincoat, pulled her hair into a low, tight bun, and grabbed her backpack. If she was careful, maybe she could save both Tia's life *and* her own. Just in case, though, she left a note behind for Bill and

Ryker, explaining everything.

"Sorry, girl, but you've got to stay here," she told Smutti when the dog tried to follow her from the room. Leaning down, she kissed the long black nose and whispered goodbye before slipping out into the hallway.

Zaylie quietly walked past Bill and Ryker's rooms, hoping they wouldn't choose that very moment to go looking for a vending machine. Once she was in the clear, she took the stairs and was outside in seconds. She ran through the rain and hopped into the rental car, feeling grateful that the rental company had given them two sets of keys. After putting the address into her phone's GPS, she backed out of the parking space and took off.

The night was dark, and thunder rumbled loudly overhead. Sporadic flashes of lightning lit the way in front of her as she turned off the main highway and headed down an old, narrow road. Overgrown trees grew wildly on either side, and Zaylie wondered how long it had been since anyone came down here. Glancing at her GPS, she saw that her final destination was only a quarter mile away.

Pulling over, Zaylie turned off the engine and got out of the car. She tucked her gun into her back pocket, grabbed a flashlight, and swung the backpack around her shoulders. Rain dripped from the hood of her raincoat, and as she headed off down the road, she was more grateful than ever for her waterproof hiking boots.

She was getting closer. The storm hadn't let up one bit, and when a flash of lightning lit up an old, abandoned gas station up ahead, she knew she was almost there. Stepping off the road, Zaylie walked into the dark woods to her left and slowly made her way toward the building. Twigs and small branches snapped loudly beneath her feet, and for once, Zaylie was glad it was raining, as it helped to mask the sound. She kept her hand over the flashlight's beam so that only a small stream of light bled through her fingers and allowed her to see where she was going. Her heart pounded as she drew closer. Was she really going through with this?

Suddenly, a mighty clap of thunder shook the ground beneath her feet, and a massive owl flew from the trees above her head. With a gasp, Zaylie crouched down for a moment, her legs trembling. She hated being alone in the dark, and she had to force herself to breathe deeply.

You can do this, she told herself. *You're so close.*

Rising once again, Zaylie continued on. Just a few more feet, and she would reach a break in the trees, which led directly to the back of the gas station. She moved forward and then stopped, clicking off her flashlight. She stood there, silently searching the darkness and wondering where he was. She knew he was out here somewhere; he wouldn't be waiting inside like a sitting duck. She suspected he was in the woods across the street, waiting for her to drive up. Could she possibly sneak in through the back way and get Tia out without him knowing?

Taking a deep breath, Zaylie stepped from the cover of the trees and hurried toward the back door. She reached it, and with a trembling hand, she slowly turned the knob. It was unlocked. Was that a good sign, or did it mean he'd known she would come in the back way and was waiting for her inside? The door slowly opened, and Zaylie stepped inside, gun in hand. The rain beat loudly against the building and blew inside through busted window panes. She stood still for a moment, listening for any sound other than that of the storm. She could barely see in the darkness, so she clicked her flashlight back on, but kept her hand over the beam.

The room had apparently once been the supply room; empty cartons of beer and opened packages of chips were scattered sporadically about. A large, lone rat stood in one of the far corners, eyeing Zaylie with a steely eye as it tore into an old bag of pretzels.

"Stay away from me, and I'll stay away from you," Zaylie whispered, making sure to keep her distance from the creature.

A closed door, which Zaylie assumed led out into the main room, stood only a few feet away. Was that where he was keeping Tia? Inching forward, she overlooked the empty soup can that rested in her path. Her foot connected with the metal container, and she froze, her heart kicking into overdrive as the can rattled loudly across the floor.

Suddenly, the door before her burst open, and a large figure emerged. With a scream, Zaylie jumped back, the sound of her gun as it fired blending in with a loud crack of thunder. The figure paused for only a brief second before reaching out to grab her by the arm. Her gun and flashlight fell to the floor, leaving the man's face covered in shadows.

Zaylie kicked and struggled, trying to pull away from his firm grip. Why had she come here by herself? Did she really think she was capable of defending herself against a deranged killer? Fear swirled around her like a thick cloud of smoke, and she began to kick harder.

"Zaylie, stop kicking me!"

The familiar voice finally broke through the panicked chatter in her brain, and she stopped.

"R-Ryker?" she stammered.

Releasing her arm, Ryker reached down for the flashlight and shined it on his face. Zaylie breathed a sigh of relief and tried to calm the erratic racing of her heart.

"Are you okay?" he asked. "What on earth is going on?"

Just then, over the pounding of the rain, they heard the sound of an engine roaring to life. They both hurried through the building and peered out one of the front windows. Racing off down the road were the glowing taillights of a retreating vehicle, and Zaylie moaned with frustration.

"He got away," she said with a sigh.

"He? As in the killer?" Ryker asked in disbelief.

Zaylie nodded. "Yes," she replied, proceeding to explained what had happened. "How did you know I was here?"

"I'd gone to my truck to look for my phone charger when I saw you sneaking out," he said. "So, I followed you. I stayed far enough behind that I didn't know where you went after you ditched your car on the side of the road, so I got out and walked. I'd just come in through the front door when I heard that loud clatter. Zaylie, what on earth were you thinking? You could have been killed."

Moving her eyes away from Ryker's piercing gaze, Zaylie opened her mouth to explain when she spotted something in the flashlight's beam.

"Ryker, what is that?" she whispered.

Ryker turned to look, pointing his flashlight directly at the object. They both took a step closer, and a gasp passed their lips at the same time. It was the body of a young woman, and by the blank look in her wide open eyes, it was obvious she was dead.

CHAPTER 17

When Bill arrived, along with the sheriff and FBI agents, he was livid.

"Do you realize you could be dead right now if Ryker hadn't followed you?" he asked her, his face red. "I can't believe you did something so careless and irresponsible."

Zaylie felt like she was ten again, but she didn't let Bill's lecture get to her; she knew he was just worried about her.

"I didn't know what else to do," she said, showing him the email she'd received. "I was afraid he'd kill Tia if I didn't do what he said."

"Well, she's dead anyway, and we might have caught this guy if you'd just called us," Ellington spoke up.

Zaylie's face flushed. "You're right," she said, turning to look at him. "I'm sorry. I thought I was doing the right thing."

Pursing his lips, Ellington turned without another word and got back to work. They stayed for another hour or so as Zaylie gave her full statement, and then they went back to the hotel. It was nearly two o'clock in the morning by the time they made it back, and Zaylie was exhausted. After taking a quick shower to wash off the grime of the night, she fell into bed and cried herself to sleep.

The next morning, Zaylie packed her few belongings and met Ryker and Bill downstairs. There was no point in continuing to stay, and Bill had gotten them return flights home.

"Ryker, you wouldn't like to have a travel companion with you as you drive home, would you?" Zaylie asked as he headed toward his truck.

Stopping, he turned to look at her in surprise. "I thought you already had an airline ticket?" he asked.

Zaylie pointed to Smutti and smiled. "I wasn't referring to myself," she replied. "It's not super comfortable for her in those planes; she'd be able to get more rest if she rode with you."

Eyeing the large dog skeptically, Ryker asked, "What do I do if she, you know, has to go potty?"

"She won't," Zaylie replied with a laugh. "I'll walk her now before you leave, and she'll be good until you get home. Just in case, though, I'll give you a leash."

"Okay, then," he replied. "I'm sorry I don't have room for all three of you."

"It's fine." Zaylie shrugged. "Your truck is a work truck and you didn't have time to unpack it before you left. I understand."

Zaylie walked Smutti around for a few moments and then led her over to Ryker's truck. After Smutti jumped into the passenger seat, Zaylie leaned around the large dog to look at Ryker.

"Thank you for doing this, and also for what you did last night," she told him. "Bill was right; if not for you, I'd most likely be dead right now. For all we know, you saved my life."

Ryker draped an arm over the steering wheel and nodded. "You're welcome. I'm glad your grandmother talked me into coming." With a twinkle coming into his eyes, he added, "You know, it almost seems like we're becoming friends."

Her lips twitching, Zaylie ignored his last comment and kissed Smutti on the nose. "Be good for Ryker, okay? Try not to give him too much grief."

Ryker's eyebrows shot up. "Uh, just what kind of grief could she give me?"

With a sly grin, Zaylie waved to him and said, "Bye now. Drive safe," and shut the door.

By the time Zaylie and Bill got to the airport, checked in, and made it through security, it was almost noon. The Atlanta airport was always busy and full of travelers, and today was no exception. When they arrived at their gate, they were both starving.

"What do you want to eat?" Bill asked. "There are a lot of options, and…well, what do you know? There's Cameron Sterling."

Zaylie blinked, and then turned to look in the direction Bill's gaze was pointed. Sitting in one of the chairs at their gate was a very distinguished-looking man wearing a gray suit and a very expensive pair of black Ferragamo shoes. He was extremely handsome, in a sleek and stylish Brad Pitt sort of way. His blonde hair was cut short on the sides, while the top was thick and voluminous and held in place with a firm styling balm. Zaylie noticed several women giving him the eye, but he ignored them all as he flipped coolly through a magazine.

"Cameron, what a surprise," Bill said as he approached the younger man.

Cameron looked up, his blue eyes widening slightly. "Bill Harper," he said, standing to shake Bill's hand. "What are you doing here?"

Bill motioned to Zaylie, who had stepped up behind him, and said, "We flew up here a couple of days ago for official business. Cameron, do you know Zaylie Layne?"

Turning to direct his piercing gaze at Zaylie, Cameron didn't immediately respond, and Zaylie had the impression that he *did* somehow know her.

"No, I don't believe I've ever had the pleasure," he finally replied with a smooth, charming smile. Reaching out to take her hand, he said, "It's nice to meet you, Miss Layne."

"I believe you knew my sister," Zaylie said, not wasting any time. Who knew when she'd get such a perfect chance to talk to him again.

Cameron raised his eyebrows. "Oh?"

"Yes." Zaylie nodded. "Her name was Zoe."

Cameron tilted his head to the side and looked

down at the ground, as if deep in thought. After a moment, he snapped his fingers and said, "Ah, yes, I believe I *do* remember her! She was murdered some years back, wasn't she?"

Zaylie flinched at his choice of words. No matter how often she heard them, she never seemed to be prepared to hear them.

"That's right," Bill spoke up. "We never found her killer."

Cameron shook his head with a *tsk.* "What a shame," he murmured. "I didn't know her very well, but I remember that she was a lovely girl."

Zaylie's eyes narrowed, but before she could respond, Bill asked, "Why are *you* here, Cameron?"

Pushing his hands into the pockets of his pants, Cameron rocked back onto his heels and said, "I'm here on business. I would normally have used my own private jet, but it's currently under repair. Hopefully, I won't have to fly like this again, though; these airports are so hectic."

The poor man, having to fly with the rest of us commoners, Zaylie thought, inwardly rolling her eyes.

Bill cleared his throat and said, "Yes, well, I'm going to grab something to eat before it's time to board. Zaylie, are you coming?"

Zaylie shook her head. Her stomach was pinching from hunger, but she wasn't going to miss this opportunity to question Cameron further.

After Bill walked away, Cameron sat down and

Zaylie took the seat next to his. "I hope you don't mind if I join you?" she asked.

With a dazzling smile, Cameron shook his head and said, "Not at all."

"I saw an old friend of yours the other day," she stated.

Cameron raised his eyebrows curiously. "Oh?" he asked.

"Yes," Zaylie replied. "Erica Harper. She was Zoe's best friend."

"I haven't seen Erica in ages," he stated, setting the magazine he'd been reading on a nearby table. "How is she?"

"Good," Zaylie said. "She's moved back to the island with her husband, Devon. I understand the two of you used to be good friends."

Cameron looked away and shifted in his seat. "Yes, we were. I haven't seen him in years, though."

Zaylie tilted her head. "I'm surprised at that," she said, watching him closely. "From the way Erica talked, y'all were thick as thieves. She said you held some pretty wild parties back in the day, too."

Cameron chuckled. "It sounds like all you two did was talk about me," he said. Leaning his elbow on the armrest that divided their seats, he leaned toward Zaylie and asked, "Did she say anything else about me?"

Zaylie nodded. Their faces were only inches apart, and she could feel the jealous stares of every woman within thirty feet. "Actually, she did," she replied slowly. "She said when you came on to Zoe once, she slapped you and you slapped her back."

An odd look passed over Cameron's face, one that Zaylie couldn't identify. He sat back, putting some space between them, and reached up to loosen the tie around his neck. After a moment, he said in a low tone, "That was a long time ago."

Zaylie's eyes narrowed. Did she detect a hint of remorse in his voice? Or was he simply the type who could talk his way out of anything?

"Where were you the night my sister died?" she asked, pushing away a nagging feeling that was warning her not to press too far.

Cameron's striking blue gaze swept back to stare at Zaylie's face. His jaw clenching, he said, "I don't remember."

Before Zaylie could said anything else, he stood to his feet and said stiffly, "I think Bill's suggestion of grabbing a bite to eat before takeoff was a good idea, so please excuse me."

Zaylie watched as Cameron hurried off, and she knew the next time she saw him would be as he boarded ahead of her into first class. She sat back in her chair and sighed, wondering if she'd pushed too hard. Ryker had warned her about him, but how else was she to find answers if she didn't ask the difficult questions? If only she had Rita's charming, friendly personality, perhaps she'd be making better progress.

Zaylie's phone chimed, and her heart caught when she saw it was a new email alert. When she unlocked her phone, though, she realized it was just spam. She closed her phone and put it back into her purse, feeling like the weight of the world was on her shoulders. Tia's death was her fault; she knew that. He was angry with her for interfering in Lauren's case and was punishing her for it. Would he do it again? How many more women would die because of her?

CHAPTER 18

When Zaylie arrived back home, she was exhausted. The last two days had taken their toll, and all she wanted was to take a hot shower and go to bed. Ryker had just arrived with Smutti when Zaylie pulled up, and she was glad the two had made the trip in one piece.

"Hey, you," Zaylie said with a smile as Smutti bounded toward her, tail wagging. "It's only been a few hours since you saw me, you know."

"She makes a pretty good travel companion," Ryker stated as he climbed from his truck. "Other than the time I almost lost her at the gas station, we had no problems at all."

Zaylie's head jerked up as she looked at him with wide, worried eyes. "You...you almost *lost* her?"

With a grin, Ryker winked at her and said, "That was payback for the little grief speech you gave before we left Alpharetta."

Zaylie sighed and shook her head. "You should be ashamed of yourself. I nearly had a heart attack."

"Oh, honey, I'm so glad you're back!"

Zaylie looked up to see Gran hurrying out the front door with open arms. smiled, Zaylie stepped into her grandmother's embrace and said,

"Thanks, Gran. It's good to be home."

"I'll see you two in the morning," Ryker said, waving goodbye as he climbed into his truck and drove away.

"You look so tired," Gran said, patting Zaylie on the back as they walked inside. "Did y'all find the missing girl?"

"She's dead, Gran," Zaylie replied, tears filling her eyes. "He killed her."

Her face filling with sympathy, Gran shook her head and said, "I'm so sorry. Her poor family." Looking closely at her granddaughter, she added, "It's not your fault, Zaylie. You didn't cause this."

How was it that Gran always seemed to be able to read her mind? Unable to hold back the tears, Zaylie stepped into her grandmother's warm embrace and cried. After her mom left, Gran was the only mother she'd had, and her comforting presence was like a balm for Zaylie's troubled spirit.

"Why don't you go upstairs and lie down?" Gran asked, pulling back to wipe the tears gently from Zaylie's face. "I'll make you a cup of chamomile tea to help you relax."

Zaylie nodded, and after taking a hot shower, she drank the tea and fell into bed.

Three hours later, Zaylie woke to the sound of her phone vibrating. The sun was going down, and the aroma of Gran cooking supper was wafting up into her room. Sitting up, Zaylie grabbed her phone, her heart sinking when she saw it was her father. She knew he'd want to know everything that had happened, and she didn't feel like discussing it right now.

"Hi, Dad," she said, forcing a bit of cheer into her voice. "How are you? Still in Wyoming?"

"Yes, we're in Cody right now," he replied. "Zaylie, I just talked to Bill."

Oh, boy, Zaylie groaned inwardly. No matter how old she got, she still hated getting lectured by her father.

"Dad, I know I should have used more sense, but I thought I was doing the right thing…" she began but was quickly interrupted.

"You thought going out to meet a kidnapper and killer in the middle of the night by yourself was the right thing?" Her dad sighed. "Zaylie, you need to stop this. I've already lost one daughter; I don't want to lose another."

"It's the same guy, Dad," Zaylie told him. "It's Zoe's killer."

"Then let the professionals handle it," he stated. "It's not your responsibility to find your sister's killer."

Zaylie sat in silence for a moment, struggling with her emotions. No matter what her dad said, she felt like it *was* her responsibility. If she'd done more, if she'd been able to remember everything that happened all those years ago, maybe they could have saved Zoe.

"Zaylie? Are you okay?"

Her dad's voice broke through the silence, and Zaylie was drawn from the dark depths of her thoughts.

"Yeah," she replied hoarsely. Clearing her throat, she added, "I can't promise to leave this alone, Dad, but I *will* be more careful. I can promise you that."

Her dad sighed, and she could picture him shaking his head. "Okay, honey."

Zaylie changed the conversation then, and they talked about his trip and her stepmom. It seemed the two of them were having a wonderful time, and Zaylie was happy for them.

Once Zaylie was off the phone, she went downstairs to help Gran finish making supper. Much to her surprise, Ryker was sitting at the kitchen counter, slicing a loaf of ciabatta bread.

"I thought you weren't coming back 'til tomorrow?" Zaylie asked when she saw him.

Ryker looked over at her. "A customer called earlier to ask if I could come out tomorrow for an emergency repair. Mrs. Ferguson said it was perfectly alright to hold off on the renovations here for a few days, so I stopped by to pick up some tools I'd left here."

"And, of course, I asked him to stay for supper," Gran interjected, her eyes twinkling with pleasure.

"And, of course, I said yes," Ryker said, smiling at Gran.

"Never say no to Gran's spaghetti," Zaylie said when she spotted the noodles boiling on the stove.

"What can I do to help?"

"You can set the table," Gran replied. "It's almost ready."

The three of them enjoyed a nice supper together. Ryker told a few stories from his days in the Navy, and Gran even chimed in with a few stories of her own from her childhood. When Ryker asked about the painting of Great Aunt Azalea, Gran's face became solemn.

"That's Azalea," she told him. "She was Zaylie's father's aunt and my very best friend. Wasn't she beautiful? I have always thought that Zaylie here looks just like her."

Ryker looked at Zaylie and nodded. "I can certainly see the resemblance." With a sly grin, he added, "I doubt Azalea was as stubborn, though."

Gran laughed, and Zaylie's face flushed.

"Oh, she was every bit as stubborn," Gran replied. "When we were girls, she could talk me into just about anything."

"If the truth be known, it was probably the other way around," Zaylie stated with a laugh.

Gran swatted at Zaylie with her napkin. "You be quiet, young lady."

Laughing, Ryker took a sip of his sweet tea and asked, "What ever happened to Azalea?"

Gran leaned back against her chair and sighed. "No one knows," she said, shaking her head sadly. "Her father and his business partners owned a bank here in town. After some terrible things happened, Azalea simply disappeared. We were all heartbroken."

Zaylie stared at Gran in surprise. Any time she'd tried to ask about Azalea, Gran's responses were always very vague. Zaylie had never even heard about her Great Grandfather owning a bank.

"What were the terrible things that happened?" she wanted to know.

Before Gran could answer, a scratching sound, followed by a low whine, sounded at the back door. Wondering what was wrong with Smutti, Zaylie got up to let her dog inside. As soon as she opened the back door, she gasped. Smutti was wheezing and stumbling around on the back deck, and white foam was quickly forming around her mouth.

"Smutti!" she cried, rushing to her dog's side.

Hearing the panicked tone in her voice, Ryker hurried outside to see what had happened. Kneeling at Smutti's side, it didn't take him long to come to a conclusion.

"Zaylie, she's been poisoned."

CHAPTER 19

Ryker scooped Smutti into his arms and hurried around to the front of the house. Zaylie raced inside on trembling legs, grabbed her purse, and ran out front to meet him.

"Here, you drive," she said, thrusting her keys into his waiting hand as she climbed into the back seat of her car next to Smutti.

The drive to the emergency vet clinic felt like an eternity. Smutti was breathing, but her heart rate was fast and she kept whining softly. As tears splashed from her eyes, Zaylie held Smutti's head in her lap and gently rubbed her behind the ears. What would she do if something happened to her dog?

"Hold on, girl," she whispered. "We're almost there."

It took nearly ten minutes to reach the clinic, and when they hurried inside, they were greeted by a young girl behind the desk.

"What happened?" she immediately asked.

"We think she was poisoned," Zaylie said in a shaky voice.

Nodding, the girl motioned for them to follow her. "Bring her back here, please," she said to Ryker as she led them into the operating room. "Do you know what she ingested?"

"No," Zaylie replied, shaking her head. "She was in the backyard by herself."

Ryker laid Smutti on one of the tables, and the girl said, "If y'all will wait out front, I'll get the veterinarian who is on call and then come back out to get your name and information."

"It's going to be okay, sweet girl," Zaylie said, kissing Smutti's nose. Her breathing had grown more labored, and her eyes were no longer open. Zaylie felt like her heart was breaking as Ryker took her hand and pulled her from the room, and when the door shut behind them, she wondered if she would ever see Smutti again.

Twenty minutes passed, and then an hour. Zaylie paced back and forth around the waiting room, her stomach in knots. Gran kept texting for updates, but unfortunately, there were none yet.

"How could this have happened?" Zaylie asked, voicing the question both to Ryker and herself. "Do you think it was intentional?"

"I don't know." Ryker sighed, shaking his head as he leaned his elbows onto his knees.

Nearly two hours later, the door finally opened, and Zaylie turned to face the doctor, anxious to hear what he had to say. What she hadn't been prepared for was to come face to face with someone from her past.

Recognition flitting across his face, he stopped in his tracks and blinked. "Zaylie," he said, his familiar, raspy voice filled with surprise.

Zaylie hadn't seen Micah Pierce since Spring

Break over ten years ago. She'd heard he'd left the island and moved to North Carolina to go to veterinary school, but she didn't know he'd come back home.

"It's good to see you again," he added, taking a small step forward.

He was even more handsome than she remembered. His curly brown hair was cut shorter than it used to be, and his blue eyes were just as bright and clear as they ever were. He'd always been tall, but she didn't fail to notice that he'd filled out quite nicely.

Ryker cleared his throat loudly, and with a flush of heat on her cheeks, Zaylie suddenly realized she was staring. Smiling tightly, she said, "Yes, it's good to see you again, too." Her mind then turned to the reason they were there, and she immediately asked about Smutti.

"She's going to be just fine," Micah assured her. "I'm guessing she vomited some of it up before you found her, but it appears that the drug was a strong one. I would like to keep her overnight, just to make sure everything is okay."

Relief flooded over Zaylie like a tidal wave, and tears immediately filled her eyes.

"Thank you so much," she said hoarsely, wiping the moisture from her eyes. "You have no idea how grateful I am."

Micah nodded. "We'll call you tomorrow afternoon and let you know when to come pick her up," he said. "My partner will be working tomorrow, so you'll most likely see him."

Micah let Zaylie see Smutti for a few minutes, and then she and Ryker left. The drive home was mostly silent as Zaylie absently twirled her hair around her finger and gazed out the window, deep in thought. Seeing Micah again had been a huge surprise, and she wasn't certain how she felt about it. He was the first boy she'd ever dated, and at sixteen, she'd thought he would be the last. He'd helped her cope with so many of her insecurities over losing her sister and mother. They dated for two years and she remembered being madly in love with him...until he left for college and cheated on her.

"I'll bet it was strange to see Micah again," Ryker stated, breaking her thoughts.

Zaylie nodded. "Yeah. I didn't know he'd moved back."

Ryker glanced at her in surprise. "Your grandmother didn't tell you?" he asked.

"No, she didn't," Zaylie replied, her mind already going over the conversation she planned to have with Gran as soon as she got home.

"Are...are you okay?"

The hesitation in Ryker's voice made Zaylie smile. Rita must have told him how heartbroken she'd been after the break-up with Micah.

"You mean about Smutti?" she asked, looking over at him innocently.

"Well, that too," he replied. Clearing his throat, he added, "But also about Micah."

"It feels weird to see Micah again after all these years," she said, not intending to go into anymore detail than that. "As for Smutti, I'm terribly upset. Will you help me search the property when we get back? If I can find that she was intentionally poisoned, that's got to mean only one thing."

"That your sister's killer thought he'd try a new tactic to get to you?"

"Exactly." Zaylie shivered. "The thought of him being on our property terrifies me. What if he'd tried to hurt Gran instead? I've got to tell Bill about this."

When they arrived back home, Zaylie grabbed a flashlight from her glove compartment and they began searching the grounds. Crickets and cicadas chirped loudly from the marsh and surrounding trees, and the moon shone brightly overhead. The night air was warm and humid, and Zaylie swatted at a swarm of sand gnats as she ducked out of their way.

"Over there," Ryker said, pointing to something on the ground near the gazebo.

Aiming the beam of the flashlight in that direction, Zaylie and Ryker stepped closer. They both squatted down for a better look, but it was obvious; several pieces of raw meat lay on the ground, and a powdery white substance was sprinkled on top.

"Well, this confirms it," Ryker stated in a heavy tone. "Smutti's poisoning was intentional."

Zaylie immediately called Bill, and within twenty minutes, several officers were on the premises. They bagged the meat and walked all around the area, carefully searching the ground for clues.

"Do y'all keep the gate at the entrance of the driveway locked?" Bill asked.

"Only at night," Zaylie replied, tucking a stray piece of auburn hair behind her ear.

"Y'all need to consider putting up cameras," he said, coming to stand beside her. "On a large piece of property such as this, I always recommend having some sort of security, especially since you don't have any close neighbors."

"That is a great idea," she replied, nodding. "I don't know why I haven't thought of that before."

"A security system wouldn't be a bad idea either," he told her.

"I agree," Zaylie said. "I'll call Devon and ask how soon he can get it done."

"Be careful until then, Zaylie," Bill told her. "This guy is getting pretty bold."

Zaylie nodded, her stomach clenching nervously. "We'll do our best."

"We can't find anything," one of the officers told Bill.

With a sigh, Bill said, "Okay. We'll need to come back out tomorrow and search again in the daylight." Turning back to Zaylie, he added, "We'll get that meat tested ASAP, but I don't know how much help that will be. Unless it's an unusual drug that can be more easily traced."

"I understand," Zaylie replied. Touching Bill on the arm, she said, "Thanks for always having our backs."

Bill patted her hand and then told his men to pack up and head out. Once they were all gone, Zaylie went inside the house to find Ryker sitting with Gran in the kitchen.

"Zaylie, Ryker is going to stay with us until we can get an alarm system installed," Gran stated.

Zaylie raised her eyebrows. "Oh...okay," she stammered.

"Don't worry, I'm going to sleep on the sofa," he told her with a wink.

Zaylie gave him a look and, ignoring his statement, asked, "I thought you had an emergency customer you had to see about this weekend?"

"I can still go by his house in the morning," he replied with a shrug.

Gran cleared her throat loudly. "It was very nice of Ryker to offer to stay and look out for us, wasn't it?" she asked, giving Zaylie a very pointed look.

"Yes, it was," Zaylie replied, relaxing a bit. With a smile, she looked at Ryker and said sincerely, "Thank you, Ryker. Not just for staying, but also for all of your help. Smutti might not have made it if you hadn't been here tonight."

Ryker waved a hand in the air and said, "You're

very welcome."

A bit later, as Zaylie readied herself for bed, thoughts of the day kept rolling through her mind. She thought of Micah and sighed, realizing she'd forgotten to ask Gran about him. She wondered if he was married or had any children and found herself thinking back to the days when they were young and in love.

As she flipped off the bathroom light and walked into her bedroom, Zaylie yawned wearily. She glanced around the room, thinking about Smutti and how much she missed her comforting presence. It would be wonderful to have her back home in less than twenty-four hours.

She walked to the window and parted the curtains to look outside. The floodlights were on, illuminating the backyard below, but the beams only went so far. The shadows beyond the light were what was most concerning, and she found herself wondering if anyone was lurking in those shadows along the tree line.

Pulling the curtains back together, she fought off a chill of foreboding and crawled into bed. She'd never thought she would say this, but she was very grateful that Ryker Steele was downstairs. As she slowly drifted off to sleep, she thanked God that Ryker had stopped by that evening to get his tools.

Less than an hour later, something awakened her, but Zaylie wasn't sure what. She sat up in bed and looked at the clock; it was a little after midnight. Was she simply dreaming?

There it was again; a slight thumping sound was coming from beneath her window. Throwing back the covers, Zaylie climbed out of bed and hurried over to her window to look out. The backyard was bathed in light, but the area just below her window was covered in darkness. Grabbing her robe, Zaylie slid it on and hurried downstairs.

The wood floor was cold beneath her bare feet, and as Zaylie slid quietly down the stairs, she inwardly berated herself for not grabbing a flashlight first. The bottom floor was dark and still; the only sound to be heard was what now sounded like a rustling in the bushes. Feeling her way along the wall toward the living room, Zaylie tried not to panic. It was probably just an animal. Right?

Suddenly, Zaylie's fingers connected with a warm body, and she froze. When a large hand grabbed her by the arm, she opened her mouth to scream but stopped when Ryker's familiar voice hissed through the silence.

"Zaylie, it's me."

Collapsing against the wall, Zaylie took a deep breath and tried to control the trembling in her body. After taking a moment to gather herself, she asked in a hoarse whisper, "D-do you hear that noise?"

"I hear it," he replied, his voice steady.

"Is Gran okay?" she wanted to know.

"Yes," he said. "I checked on her just now and she's sleeping."

The rustling grew louder, and Zaylie's heart

accelerated once again. Surely, the killer hadn't returned? Perhaps that had been his plan all along; get Smutti out of the way first and then make his move. But didn't he see Ryker's truck parked in the driveway?

"I tried looking out the back window, but it's not close enough to where the noise is coming from," Ryker stated. "So, I'm going outside to check things out. Lock the door behind me, and if I'm not back in five minutes, call the police."

Zaylie followed him toward the back of the house, her legs shaking so badly she could hardly walk. When she told him she hadn't brought her phone along, he handed her his phone.

"Ryker, don't go out there," she begged when the rustling turned back into a loud thump. "He's just trying to lure you out of the house."

"Hey, I can take care of myself, remember?" Ryker asked, reaching out to touch her arm. "Don't worry. I'll be back before you know it."

Before she could think of another way to stop him, he slipped out the back door and was gone. With jerky movements, Zaylie locked the door behind him and waited.

The clock that hung over the stove seemed to tick much slower than usual. Zaylie clutched Ryker's phone in her hand and wondered if she should go ahead and call the police. Could they even get here in time? Oh, why hadn't she asked Bill to leave an officer stationed outside until they could get the security system installed?

Tick tock, tick tock. The clock was growing louder and louder, and the darkness was starting to close in around her. Why wasn't Ryker back yet? And why hadn't she heard a commotion coming from outside? Had the killer simply hit him on the head, rendering him unconscious, and was about to break through one of the windows?

Just then, Zaylie heard the sound of footsteps approaching, and her heart began beating double-time. She took a step backward, away from the door, and stared at it. Was it Ryker, or someone else? She unlocked the cell phone and pulled up the dial screen, ready to punch in 911 at any second.

Knock, knock, knock.

Three firm thumps sounded on the back door, and Zaylie jerked, nearly dropping the phone. She looked down at the bright screen, the numbers blurring before her eyes. She could barely breathe or think, but she raised a trembling finger toward the 9 and tapped it.

"Zaylie? Are you going to let me in?"

Blinking, Zaylie hurriedly unlocked the door and let Ryker back inside. It was all she could do not to throw her arms around his neck when she found him completely unscathed.

"It was an armadillo," he said, shaking his head. "I chased it off. You okay?"

Zaylie handed him his phone and sighed. "I doubt I'll sleep the rest of the night, but I'm just peachy."

Ryker chuckled, his deep voice rumbling in the

darkness as they made their way back through the house. "Glad I was here?" he asked.

Stopping at the stairs, Zaylie looked back at his silhouette and nodded. "Very glad," she said softly before hurrying back up the stairs.

CHAPTER 20

The next morning, Zaylie was brushing her teeth when her cell phone rang. Snatching it up in the hope that it was the vet, she blinked in surprise when she heard Micah's voice.

"My partner couldn't come in today," he explained, "so I'm filling in for him. Smutti is doing great; she had a good night and ate this morning with no problem. Would it be okay if I brought her to you around noon? I never got the chance to visit the old place before, you know, and I'd love to see if it's as beautiful as everyone says."

Zaylie agreed, and after they hung up, she called Devon about the security system.

"I can come by to take a look this afternoon," he told her.

Thanking him, she disconnected the call, threw on a black and white striped dress, and headed downstairs. She tried to ignore the fact that she was a little nervous about Micah's visit and instead focused on how excited she was that Smutti was well enough to return home.

When she arrived downstairs, Ryker was already gone and Gran was in the kitchen. Not bothering to mention what happened the night before, Zaylie told her about Smutti.

"I'm so glad she's going to be okay," Gran said in a

relieved tone as she sat down at the table with her newspaper. "I was so worried about her."

"Me, too," Zaylie said as she fixed herself a cup of coffee. "Hey, why didn't you tell me Micah had moved back to the island?"

Gran looked up from her newspaper, the glasses perched on the end of her nose slowly slipping downward. "Oh, well, I just thought I'd wait awhile," she stammered.

"Why?" Zaylie wanted to know, placing a hand on her hip.

The glasses fell off Gran's nose and she caught them without a flinch. Tapping them on the edge of the counter, she wiggled in her chair and said, "I was afraid you wouldn't want to come back if you knew he was here."

Zaylie sighed. "I still would have come back, Gran. I'm not going to let his presence here ruin my love for the island. A warning would have been nice, though."

Gran looked down dismally and said, "I'm sorry, honey. You're right; I should have told you."

Thinking there was more to it than that, Zaylie narrowed her eyes and asked, "Is that why you've been so pushy with Ryker?"

Gran looked up at Zaylie innocently. "What do you mean?" she asked, shifting in her chair once again.

"You know exactly what I mean," Zaylie stated. "Were you hoping I'd form an attachment to Ryker so that Micah's presence wouldn't bother me so much?"

"So, his presence *does* bother you!" Gran gasped, ignoring Zaylie's question. Slapping her hand lightly against the countertop, she said, "Zaylie Layne, don't you dare consider going back to that man after the way he broke your heart."

Zaylie rolled her eyes. "Nice deflection," she said drolly. "Look, Gran, even if Micah was interested in me, I'm not planning to go back down that road again."

Pursing her lips, Gran picked up her newspaper again and muttered, "I hope not."

Zaylie shook her head and smiled. Her grandmother meant well, she knew that, but sometimes that woman could drive a body to distraction.

After breakfast, Zaylie drove down to the local Farmers Market. She bought two baskets full of fresh fruit and vegetables, a dozen eggs, some freshly baked bread, some coffee, and honey. She loved supporting local businesses, and everything was always so fresh and delicious. As she headed toward her car, she realized it was a few minutes past eleven. Picking up her pace, she hurried the rest of the way. She didn't plan to be late for Smutti's arrival back home.

Zaylie had just turned out onto the main road when her car started to vibrate. Frowning, she slowed down and pulled into the right-hand lane just as a loud *boom* burst through the air and her car jerked roughly to one side. With a gasp, she clutched the steering wheel tightly in both hands and managed to pull the car to a stop in the emergency lane.

Stepping from the car, Zaylie walked slowly around the vehicle, moaning when she spotted the flat tire. She knew how to change a tire, but it had been so long since her dad taught her that she wasn't certain she could remember everything. Glancing down at her watch, she sighed. It was eleven thirty.

Zaylie had just pulled the spare tire and jack from her trunk when a large truck pulled up behind her. Shielding her eyes from the bright sun, Zaylie realized the driver was Clark Schultz.

"Need some help, Miss Layne?" he asked as he climbed from the truck.

Zaylie nodded gratefully. "Yes," she replied. "If you don't mind helping me with this tire, I'd be very grateful."

"I don't mind at all," he said with a smile.

Clark quickly set about changing the tire, and when Zaylie tried to help, he said, "I'll get it, Miss Layne."

Taking the hint, Zaylie stepped off to the side and just watched. Clark was wearing an opened plaid button-up shirt with a white undershirt underneath. His face was covered with what seemed an ever-present five o'clock shadow, and his deep blue eyes stayed intently trained on the task at hand.

"Thank you for doing this, Mr. Shultz," she said,

trying to break the silence.

"You can call me Clark," he replied. "And you're very welcome."

"I don't know much about you, Clark," she stated in a friendly tone. "You've lived here your entire life?"

Clark nodded. "Yes, but I wouldn't expect you to know that," he said in a slightly gruff voice. "I was raised by my grandparents in a small house on the opposite side of the island from where you and your family lived. We were never part of the "in" circle."

Zaylie shifted uncomfortably. "Oh, I'm sorry," she said, clearing her throat. "You're also older than me, though, which might explain why I never saw much of you growing up."

Clark glanced over at her with a raised eyebrow. "I'm thirty-seven," he stated, "but I guess that could be one reason."

Zaylie blinked in surprise; he looked much older than thirty-seven. Leaning against the hood of the car, she tilted her head and asked, "Did you know my sister, Zoe?"

Clark hesitated, or perhaps Zaylie just imagined that. Without looking up, he nodded and said, "Yeah, I remember her."

"Were the two of you friends?"

Clark definitely paused then. Looking up at Zaylie, he asked bluntly, "When would I have ever gotten the chance to be friends with her?"

Zaylie shrugged, feeling a little uncomfortable at

his direct gaze. "Maybe at one of the parties she apparently used to go to," she said, glancing away.

When Clark didn't answer, Zaylie looked back at him to find that he'd returned to his work. After a moment, he said, "I was never invited to any of those parties."

"Then how did the two of you meet?" she pressed.

"I don't remember," he stated in a clipped tone. Standing to his feet, he gathered up the tools and said, "All done. That should hold until you get it to the tire shop."

Zaylie stood up straight and looked down at the spare tire in surprise. "You're already done? Wow, that was fast."

Clark returned everything to her trunk and closed the lid. "I've handled my fair share of flat tires," he said matter-of-factly. "I'll see you around, Miss Layne."

"Thank you again..." Zaylie started to say, but he was already back inside his truck. Waving to him, she stepped aside as he merged back onto the road and zoomed past her car.

As Zaylie climbed back into the driver's seat, she wondered if she'd offended Clark with her questions. Apparently, he had a chip on his shoulder over the fact that he was from a "different" side of town. Zaylie's family wasn't necessarily rich, but they had always done well for themselves, and she felt sorry for Clark. It seemed he hadn't been treated fairly by his peers growing up, and she wished she'd had the chance to be friends with him. She also wished she knew more about how he'd met Zoe. It may have just been her imagination, but it almost seemed like there was something he wasn't telling her.

As Zaylie turned down her driveway, Micah turned in behind her. Zaylie could barely control her excitement to see Smutti, and as soon as she pulled up in front of the house, she jumped from the car and waited anxiously for Micah to park. As soon as he did, she rushed over to his truck and opened the back door. Smutti jumped out and, her tail wagging back and forth like an overwrought windshield wiper, covered Zaylie in wet, slobbery kisses.

"I think she's happy to see you," Micah said with a laugh as he climbed from his truck.

"Not nearly as happy as I am to see her," Zaylie replied with a smile as she rubbed her hand along Smutti's shiny black coat. "Thank you again for everything, Micah," she said, turning to look at him. "I don't think I could stand to lose her."

"You're very welcome," he replied. Taking in his surroundings, he took a long, deep breath and asked, "Would you like to take a walk and show me around?"

"Sure." Zaylie nodded.

She took Smutti inside and rejoined Micah on the front lawn where they proceeded to walk around to the back of the house. She'd known Micah since they were kids, but since her family left the island when she was ten, he'd never been to Azalea Bluff.

She could still remember those two wonderful years they'd dated. Having a long-distance relationship at such a young age hadn't been easy, but she'd come back to stay with her grandparents as much as possible. Her grandfather used to tease her by saying Micah was the real reason she liked to visit so much, and he'd been partially right. When they broke up, though, she'd still continued to visit. She'd always been close to her mother's parents, and she missed Gramp very much.

"It's just as beautiful as everyone says," Micah commented, breathing deeply of the smell of saltwater and rose bushes as he took in their surroundings. Turning to look at Zaylie, he smiled warmly and said, "And you're even more beautiful than I remembered. It's good to see you again, Zaylie. It's been a long time."

"Yes, it has," she replied, her cheeks flushing slightly. "It's good to see you again, too. I didn't realize you'd moved back to the island."

"Yes, about four months ago," he replied, pushing his hands into the pockets of his pants. "I was originally planning on moving to a big city like Boston or Philadelphia to open my own practice, but I soon realized that wasn't the life for me. I missed my family and the easy living of the island, so I decided to just come back home."

"Good for you," she said, watching as a pelican nose-dived into the river to come back up with a full beak seconds later. "I'm sure your family is thrilled to have you back home."

"They are," he replied, nodding. "How have you been? I've heard a lot of good things about your training facility."

They continued to make small talk, and the tension between them began to relax a bit. When she finished telling him about the training center, he said, "I think you should open a second facility here."

"Gran would love that," Zaylie said with a laugh. Glancing around, she added in a softer voice, "I wouldn't mind it either. I've always loved it here."

They walked to the gazebo and sat down on the cushioned seats, the soft breeze ruffling their hair. After a moment, Micah asked, "So, are you dating anyone?"

Zaylie shook her head. "No," she replied. "My job keeps me too busy to do much dating. How about you?"

"No, I'm not dating anyone," he stated, his tone a bit tight. Zaylie looked over at him to find him staring at her with a look of...regret, perhaps?

"I'm sorry for hurting you all those years ago, Zaylie," he said after a moment, his voice low. "I know we were just kids, but I really did care about you. I hope you know that."

Zaylie glanced away, hoping to hide the sudden wave of emotion she felt over his words. Taking a deep breath, she looked back at him and said with a smile, "Thank you for the apology. You're right, though; we were just kids."

He studied her for a moment before saying, "I hope we can be friends again?"

Zaylie nodded. "Of course," she replied.

With a relieved smile, he sat back against his seat and said, "Good."

Just then, Zaylie's phone rang, and she saw Bill's name flashing across the screen. When she answered, he asked, "How is Smutti?"

"She's actually home now," Zaylie told him. "Micah said she seems to be doing just fine."

"That's great news, considering the drug found in that meat was Tramadol," he stated in a heavy tone. "We're heading your way now to check your property again."

"Okay, Bill, I'll see you in a few," she replied.

"Was that Bill Harper?" Micah asked when she disconnected the call.

"It was," Zaylie replied, sliding the phone back into her pocket. "We found some meat just over there covered in a powdery substance. Bill just said it was Tramadol. They're coming back out to see if they missed anything else."

Micah's eyes grew large. "Whoa, Tramadol?" he asked. "Smutti is lucky to be alive."

"Maybe she didn't eat much of it," Zaylie said, shivering at the thought. "I'm just so thankful you were around to help her."

Micah looked at her and smiled. "Me, too."

Slapping his knees, he stood up and said, "Well, I'd better get back to work. Bring Smutti back to see me on Monday, okay? I want to check her levels. Let me know, though, if she should start acting sick in the meantime."

"Will do." Zaylie nodded, walking with him back to his car.

Before he left, Micah suddenly pulled Zaylie into a hug and said, "It sure is good to see you again. I've missed you."

As Zaylie watched him drive away, she realized she'd missed him, too. They both missed someone who didn't exist anymore, though. A great deal had changed in the last twelve years, and as Zaylie sat on the front porch steps to wait for Bill, she felt a sense of nostalgia settle over her.

CHAPTER 21

When Bill and a couple other officers arrived, Zaylie walked the premises with them. Devon arrived shortly after and immediately began inspecting the doors and windows around the house. It was nearly one o'clock, and well over 100 degrees. The humidity was almost unbearable, and by the time they'd finished working, everyone was soaked with sweat.

"I don't understand why we didn't at least find a footprint," one officer said as he wiped his brow with the back of his hand.

Bill pulled a handkerchief from his back pocket and did the same. "Probably because it's mostly grass," he said. "The lawn was recently cut, too, so there's nowhere to really find any footprints."

"Do you think he drove in here?" Zaylie asked as they all walked back toward the house.

Bill shook his head. "I doubt it," he replied. "He probably parked out on the road somewhere and walked."

As they neared the back porch, Devon waved to them and called out, "I'm finished with the inspection, Zaylie."

Nodding, Zaylie asked, "Y'all want to come inside for some sweet tea or lemonade?"

The other officers politely declined, but Bill and Devon nodded their heads eagerly.

"I've got to make a phone call, and then I'll join y'all inside," Bill said.

Zaylie led Devon into the kitchen, and they both breathed a sigh of relief at how cool and refreshing the house felt. She could hear Gran and Smutti pattering around upstairs, and she smiled as she grabbed the two pitchers from the fridge. Having Smutti back home was so comforting, and Zaylie loved being there with Gran.

"Tea or lemonade?" Zaylie asked Devon as she grabbed some glasses from the cupboard.

"Both, if you don't mind," he replied with a smile. "I like them mixed."

As Zaylie filled the glasses with ice and poured his drink, he went over the details of the security system.

"I'll work you up a proposal and have it to you by tonight," he told her.

"I know you'll give us a fair price," she said. "How soon can you get it done?"

"I won't be able to do it until next Wednesday," he replied. "David, the guy working with me, can come out and do it on Monday, though. Will that work?"

"Yes, that would be great," she said, breathing a sigh of relief. The sooner the system was installed the better.

As she set it down on the counter in front of him, she asked, "Did Erica tell you I paid her a visit the other day?"

Devon shook his head. "No, she didn't," he replied, taking a sip of his cool drink. "That was nice of you, though. I'm sure she was happy to see you after all these years."

Zaylie leaned against the counter across from him and said, "It was nice to see her again, as well." Glancing down at her glass of lemonade, she swirled the ice around for a moment before adding, "I asked her about those parties you said she and Zoe used to attend."

Devon looked at her questioningly for a moment, and then a light came into his eyes and he said, "Ah, yes. Those were the good old days."

"She said Cameron had a thing for Zoe, and when she slapped him once for getting too handsy, he slapped her back."

Devon had been staring into his own glass as she spoke, but at Zaylie's statement, his head shot up and he stared at her in surprise. "I never knew that," he stated in a clipped tone. "Cameron and I were pretty good friends for a while, but I soon came to realize he wasn't the greatest influence."

Zaylie tilted her head to one side. "So, you're not friends anymore?" she asked.

"No," was all Devon said.

Before Zaylie could ask what happened, Bill came into the kitchen, looking for a drink. After hearing the voices downstairs, Gran soon joined them.

"Where is Smutti?" Zaylie asked.

"She's asleep in your room," Gran replied. "I think she still isn't feeling very well."

As the others began to talk and share local gossip, Zaylie went upstairs for a moment to check on Smutti. Just as Gran had said, she was curled up in her bed, fast asleep. Zaylie watched her for a moment, thinking just how different the day could be if Smutti hadn't pulled through.

The next morning, Zaylie and Gran got up early to go to church. As they were driving, Gran said, "I spoke to your mom last night."

Zaylie felt her shoulders tense. "Oh?" she asked stiffly.

Gran nodded, giving Zaylie the side-eye. "She asked about you."

Zaylie shook her head and said, "Why doesn't she just ask me herself?"

"You know how she is," Gran replied, sighing. "She'd rather beat around the bush than face something head-on. She may be my daughter, but I've never really understood her."

Zaylie didn't say anything for a moment. Instead, she thought about how difficult things had been for her family. After her mother left, she'd stayed in contact with Zaylie, but their relationship was strained. When Zaylie began trying to find Zoe's killer, things just grew worse between them. Eight years ago, it all finally came to a head. Zaylie could still remember that awful conversation as if it were yesterday.

"Why can't you just let it go?" her mother, Stephanie, asked during one of her rare visits home.

"I can't, Mom," Zaylie replied. *"Don't you want Zoe's killer to be brought to justice?"*

A hard look passed over Stephanie's face, and she snapped, "I would have much rather that happened before he became her killer."

Zaylie flinched and stepped back. She wasn't entirely certain of her mother's meaning, but she'd taken the statement personally. "You blame me, don't you?" she asked as tears of pain and frustration filled her eyes.

"Don't be ridiculous," Stephanie stated, turning away. *"You were just a child."*

"That doesn't keep you from blaming me, though," Zaylie shot back.

With a sigh, Stephanie crossed her arms and said, "No matter who is to blame, I still want you to stop this. It's too painful for all of us to have to keep reliving your sister's death because you refuse to bury the past. You're being selfish, Zaylie. Don't you see that?"

Feeling hurt and angry, Zaylie asked, "How exactly are you reliving any of it? You're never around to know what I'm doing with my time."

Her shoulders tensing, Stephanie spun back around and spat, "How dare you judge me for the way I've chosen to cope with all of this! You have no idea how it feels to lose a child."

Shaking her head, Zaylie said, "You're right, but I

168

do know how it feels to lose a sister...and a mother."

That was the last conversation she'd had with her mom. Instead of staying to talk things out, Stephanie chose to leave the room and slam the door behind her. The next morning, she was gone. She remembered telling Gran what happened afterward and how they'd both cried together.

"I guess she's just hard to understand," Zaylie finally said as they pulled into the church parking lot.

Reaching over to touch Zaylie's arm, Gran said gently, "I know what she did was inconceivable, but I do believe she loves you, honey. She just doesn't know how to show love anymore. It's like she lost part of herself when Zoe died."

Zaylie nodded, her heart heavy. "We all did, Gran," she said softly before climbing from the car.

When they walked into the church, Zaylie stopped to greet a few familiar faces. She'd attended this church as a child and had visited during every trip home, so she knew almost every member. As was typical in the Deep South, everyone asked about her parents, and Zaylie answered to the best of her ability. Her conversation with Gran about her mother still stung, and having to answer questions about a woman she hadn't spoken to in eight years was extra painful today.

The music began, and Zaylie hurried inside the sanctuary to join Gran at her pew. She'd just taken her seat when a tall figure stepped in beside her.

Turning, Zaylie saw that it was Ryker, and he was dressed to the T in his Sunday best.

"Why are you sitting with us?" she asked in surprise.

Elbowing her granddaughter for being impolite, Gran leaned around Zaylie and greeted Ryker. "My goodness, you look mighty handsome in that suit," she gushed. "Doesn't he, Zaylie?"

He did, but Zaylie wasn't going to tell *him* that.

"Gran, since you're obviously so taken with Ryker, would you like to sit by him?" Zaylie asked sweetly.

Giving Zaylie a pursed-lip look, Gran turned back around to face the pulpit and began singing.

Chuckling, Ryker leaned toward Zaylie and said, "To answer your question, my dad is out of town this weekend and I didn't want to sit all by my lonesome."

"And here I thought you were a big boy," she quipped.

"Look at you, noticing," he replied teasingly.

Zaylie turned to look at him and suddenly noticed Micah sitting just across the aisle. He was watching the two of them, and when Zaylie caught his eye, he smiled and waved. When Ryker waved back, blocking Zaylie with his arm, Micah's jaw clenched in annoyance.

"By the way, you look beautiful this morning," Ryker commented, a smirk pulling at his lips as he watched Micah turn back around to face forward.

Zaylie glanced down at the light blue, floral dress

she was wearing. She loved this color blue, and she'd always been told it complimented her hair color and skin tone.

"That's kind of you to say," she replied, and feeling a bit guilty for being rude before, she added, "You look very nice, as well."

Gran handed them both a bulletin, and Zaylie turned her attention back toward the service. The singing was lovely, and Pastor Hickman preached a stirring sermon on forgiveness. As he spoke, she felt every word pierce into her soul. The last few days had been tough, to say the least, but forgiveness was something she'd struggled with for a long time. She couldn't forgive herself for Zoe's death, or her mom for leaving. Now, she felt responsible for Tia's murder. Would she ever be able to find peace?

After church was dismissed, Micah came over to say hello. At the same time, two single ladies hurried over to flirt with Ryker. They eyed Micah a bit, too, but he paid them no attention as he spoke with Zaylie. When he took her arm and walked out with her, Ryker looked a bit annoyed but couldn't seem to get away from his fan club without being rude. Zaylie was a bit surprised at the forwardness of the two women, but she supposed they found it hard to ignore a tall, handsome ex-SEAL.

"Did you enjoy the sermon?" Micah asked as they walked outside.

Zaylie nodded, still feeling tender from the message. "Yes, I did," she replied. "It was just for me, I think."

Micah looked down at her and asked gently, "You still blame yourself, don't you?"

Zaylie didn't know how she felt about having such a personal conversation with Micah. When they were dating, he'd come to know her very well and knew the things she struggled with. Apparently, he still remembered, but things were different between them now.

Turning away from him slightly, Zaylie dug through her purse for her keys. "I guess I just have a hard time letting go of the past," she stated, her tone a bit harder than she'd intended.

When she turned back to him, she saw a look of hurt on his face and realized he thought she was referring to what he'd done.

"Micah, I..."

Before she could explain, Gran stepped outside and waved to her.

"Mrs. Gibson wants to speak to you, dear," she called.

"I'll see you later, Zaylie," Micah said.

Zaylie watched as he walked away, wondering if she should stop him. What would she say, though? That she really had forgiven him and it no longer mattered what he'd done? She couldn't say that; it simply wasn't true.

As she walked back inside to speak to Gran's old neighbor, she realized more and more just how much Pastor Hickman's message really was meant for her.

CHAPTER 22

The next morning, Zaylie was awakened once again by the sound of Ryker moving furniture downstairs. With a sigh, she rolled out of bed and took Smutti outside for a short walk around the property. When they neared the gazebo, Smutti stopped and stared for a moment with a look of wariness in her demeanor. She remembered what had happened there and was afraid to return to that particular area.

"It's okay, girl," Zaylie said, rubbing Smutti gently on the back. "It's all gone now."

As if she wanted to check for herself to make sure, Smutti moved forward and cautiously sniffed around the perimeter of the gazebo.

"Morning, you two," Gran called from the back porch. "I'm meeting Jan in town for breakfast. Want to join us?"

Zaylie shook her head and said, "No, but thank you for asking. Y'all have fun. Don't gossip too much."

Wagging a finger at her granddaughter, Gran turned and went back inside the house without another word. Zaylie grinned, knowing what a gossip Jan Booker was. She was one of Gran's oldest friends, but Zaylie couldn't help teasing her grandmother a bit.

After Gran left and Smutti finished sniffing around the yard, Zaylie went back inside to fix them both some breakfast. She'd just turned the coffeemaker on when Ryker stuck his head into the kitchen and greeted her.

"Can you come look at something?" he asked.

Nodding, Zaylie followed him through the house and into the living room where he pointed to a part of the wall that had obviously been damaged by water.

"I moved the bookcase to sand this area of the wall, but I'm afraid it's going to need much more than that," he told her. Reaching out to touch the wall, he said, "It's still damp, so this is an active leak. What room is above here?"

With a sigh, Zaylie looked upward and said, "That's my bathroom."

"Must be a pipe that's leaking," Ryker stated. "Let's go upstairs and take a look, but we may need to call in a plumber."

As they walked up the stairs, Zaylie said nonchalantly, "You seem to have a few admirers at church."

"Jealous?" Ryker asked, his eyes twinkling.

Raising an eyebrow, she replied drolly, "Oh, yes. Terribly so."

"I knew it," he responded teasingly. "I was afraid you might try to fight them off."

"I'm a lover, not a fighter," she retorted, smiling.

"Could have fooled me," he muttered, and she swatted at his arm.

When they reached her bathroom, Zaylie opened the door and stepped out of the way to let him in. As he moved forward, his large body blocked her against the door and he paused to look down at her. His black hair was ruffled, with specs of sawdust sprinkled on top, and his hazel eyes were warm as he said, "You know, I'm really glad you're back home, Zaylie Layne."

Suddenly feeling a little warm at how close they stood, Zaylie raised an eyebrow and asked, "Why? So you'd have someone to annoy?"

A grin pulled at Ryker's lips, and when he leaned forward slightly, Zaylie quickly stepped back, bumping into the door and causing it to rattle loudly against the wall.

"Yes," he replied, slowly drawing the word out, "and so the island would finally have its feisty little redhead back."

Zaylie tried to swat his arm again, but he was too fast for her this time. He dodged quickly out of the way with a laugh, and she planted her hands on her hips and stated, "My hair is auburn, thank you very much. *Not* red."

With a grin, Ryker shrugged and said, "Whatever you say."

Ryker knew she hated it when people called her a redhead, but for some reason, his teasing didn't bother her as much these days as it used to.

Still chuckling, Ryker kneeled down on his knees and got to work. After doing a bit of investigating, he came to the conclusion that her toilet was leaking.

"We'll definitely have to call a plumber," he said as they headed back downstairs. "Looks like I'll be doing more work here than I originally planned. Aren't you happy that I'll be around more?"

Before Zaylie could respond, the front door banged open and a loud voice echoed off the walls.

"Where are you all, my darlings? I've come at last to ease the dreariness of life!"

Zaylie and Ryker looked at each other in shock. There was only one person who could be *that* dramatic, but what was *she* doing here?

"Am I mistaken, or is that...?" Ryker began, only to break into a wide smile when he saw his sister standing in the doorway.

"Rita!" he and Zaylie cried at the same time as they both rushed forward to hug the dark-haired beauty.

"Oh, how grand it is to see you both again!" she exclaimed with a level of genuine exuberance that only she could pull off.

"Why didn't you tell us you were coming when we saw you last week?" Zaylie wanted to know.

Rita's black eyes sparkled as she grinned with glee, "Because I wanted it to be a surprise, silly," she stated, patting her friend on the hand. Turning to her brother, she said, "Ryker, I have a car full of suitcases and boxes. When do you want to move them into your house?"

Ryker's eyebrows shot up. "Uh...what?" he stammered.

Her eyes wide, Zaylie grabbed Rita's arm and asked, "Rita, are you moving back?"

"Yes, I decided I'm tired of life on the stage, so I took your suggestion to heart," she said with a bright smile.

"What suggestion was that?" Ryker wanted to know as he crossed his arms and eyed the two women.

"To move back and work as a drama teacher," Rita said, barely able to contain her excitement as she bounced around the foyer. "Isn't Zaylie a genius? Of course, she knows how great I am with children and that I'll be a fantastic drama teacher."

Ryker looked at Zaylie in disbelief and mouthed, "*You* told her that?"

Zaylie shrugged sheepishly. Looking at Rita, she said, "This was a really quick decision, Rita. Are you sure you did the right thing?"

"Yeah," Ryker piped in, "and what about the show? You just left them in a lurch?"

A tiny flicker of uncertainty passed through Rita's eyes, but it was gone just as quickly and she said, "My understudy is going to take my place, so it really wasn't a problem for me to leave."

Zaylie knew there was more to the story, but didn't want to pressure her friend just yet. Looping her arm through Rita's, she led her into the kitchen and, glancing over her shoulder at Ryker, she asked, "So, you'll be moving in with Ryker?"

"Well, I thought about staying with Dad until I found my own place, but he's dating what's her name and that would just be weird," Rita rattled on as she helped herself to a glass of orange juice from the fridge.

Crossing his arms, Ryker leaned against the doorframe and raised his eyebrows. "What makes you think *I'm* not dating anyone?"

Rita rolled her eyes. "Because you would have already told me," she stated matter-of-factly.

Looking between the two of them, Zaylie asked, "Your dad is dating? Why didn't anyone tell me about this?"

Rita waved a hand in the air and said, "Because we're hoping it won't last."

His lips pursing with disapproval, Ryker said, "Rita, that's not nice. Mrs. Helen is okay, and you know how lonely Dad's been since Mom died."

Zaylie's eyes widened. "Your dad is dating Helen Buchanan?" she asked in surprise.

Looking at Ryker, Rita asked indignantly, "See? Zaylie doesn't like her either."

Ryker held up his hands and said, "Okay, fine. I guess she can be a little...much sometimes."

"A little?" Zaylie laughed. "Ryker, the woman stands in her front yard and yells at any of her neighbors who dare to drive over the speed limit. She even rented one of those digital speed radar things once!"

His lips twitching, Ryker shrugged and said, "Maybe she's just overly concerned about safety. Anyway, Rita, you can't move in with me."

Rita blinked, and her mouth dropped open.

"What?" she cried. "Where am I supposed to stay? On the street?"

Cue the tears, Zaylie thought, trying to hide her laughter when Rita's eyes began to moisten.

Ryker sighed, obviously frustrated. "You know I'm in the middle of renovating my new place," he explained impatiently. "It's just not livable right now."

Reaching up to wipe her eyes, Rita sniffled, "I can't believe you would turn away your very own sister. Your very own *twin*."

Before things could get any worse between the siblings, Zaylie spoke up. "Rita, why don't you stay here with us? Gran won't mind; you know you're like another granddaughter to her. Besides, it'll be much more fun than staying at Ryker's place."

The tears magically disappeared at Zaylie's suggestion as Rita clapped her hands and squealed with delight. "Thank you, thank you!" she cried, pulling Zaylie into a hug. "You are the best."

"Thank you," Ryker mouthed behind his sister's back.

With a grin, Zaylie nodded, knowing how relieved he was. She only hoped Gran would be as happy as she'd said she would be. As loveable as Rita was, she could also be...well...a bit trying at times. But as Ryker went to retrieve Rita's bags from the car and Zaylie hurried upstairs to fix up the guest bedroom, she realized she was excited to have her best friend stay with them for a while. It would be just like old times again, and right now,

Zaylie needed the comfort that often came with familiarity.

CHAPTER 23

It was almost midnight, and Zaylie had just drifted off to sleep when a loud crash sounded from down the hall. Jerking awake, she threw the covers aside and hurried to the door with Smutti at her heels. Was someone in the house? Had someone managed to bypass the new security system?

With her heart in her throat, Zaylie slowly opened her bedroom door and peered out. The hallway was dark, and Zaylie suddenly wished she'd thought to grab a flashlight. Pushing her nose past Zaylie's legs, Smutti stepped into the hall and Zaylie followed closely behind.

Just then, Zaylie heard the music, and she stopped dead in her tracks with a sigh. Hurrying the rest of the way down the hall, she threw open Rita's bathroom door and stepped in. She wasn't prepared, though, for the sight that met her. Rita's face was covered in a green clay mask, her hair was pulled on top of her head and held in place with a hot pink silk cap, and facial products were scattered all over the floor.

Zaylie reached out and tapped Rita's phone, turning off the music. Rita, who was completely oblivious to Zaylie's presence, was on her hands and knees as she scrambled to clean up the mess.

When the music stopped, she looked up and screeched in fright when she saw Zaylie.

"Good grief, Zaylie, are you trying to give me a heart attack?" she cried, covering her chest with one hand.

"Rita, do you have any idea what time it is?" Zaylie asked, ignoring her friend's question.

Rita blinked. "Uh…late?" she asked with a sheepish expression.

Zaylie nodded. "It's almost midnight. What on earth are you doing?"

Rita grabbed the rest of her face products and stood up to dump them into a bag. "I'm sorry," she said in a flustered tone. "I guess I'm used to staying up late. Did I wake you? *Please* tell me I didn't bother Gran."

"Yes, you woke me," Zaylie stated with a sigh, "but it's not the end of the world. Unless, that is, you also woke Gran."

They both paused to listen and when they were only greeted with silence, they sighed with relief.

"I'll do better from now on," Rita promised.

"Mmm hmm," Zaylie muttered with pursed lips. "Well, good night…"

"Hey, while you're up," Rita interrupted, "I'd like to ask you something."

Turning back to face her friend, Zaylie raised a questioning eyebrow. "Yes?" she asked with a yawn.

"If you're trying to solve Zoe's murder, why haven't you searched her room?"

Zaylie blinked at the random question. "The police searched it years ago," she replied.

Rita turned the water on in the sink and began scrubbing the mask off her face. "Yeah, but have *you* searched it?" she wanted to know. "Because it looks exactly the same as it always did to me."

"You went into Zoe's room?" Zaylie asked, raising her eyebrows.

"Not really," Rita replied, her voice muffled as she buried her face in a towel. "I just peeked inside earlier, but if you ask me, it's a little creepy to just leave her things sitting around like she was coming back or something."

Zaylie bristled. "It's not **creepy**," she retorted.

"Come now, it's *Great Expectations* all over again," Rita stated matter-of-factly. "I understand keeping some of Zoe's things, but leaving her room exactly the way it was and never stepping a foot inside? It's weird."

Rita was telling the truth, even though it hurt. But how would it feel to go into Zoe's room and clean it out as if she'd never existed?

"I know you're right, but it's not really my place to do it," Zaylie finally said.

"So, talk to your parents about it," Rita replied as she smeared a thick, white moisturizer all over her face.

"I guess I could at least discuss it with Dad," Zaylie muttered.

"Atta girl," Rita replied with a dazzling smile. "Now that you're more open to the subject, why don't we go into her room now and have a look around?"

Zaylie frowned. "What for? I already told you, the police searched it years ago."

Grabbing her friend by the hand, Rita began dragging her down the hall. "Yes, but what did they know about a teenage girl?" she asked as she opened Zoe's bedroom door and turned on the light. "I used to find all sorts of nooks and crannies in my room to hide stuff from my parents when I was a kid."

While Rita breezed into the room like it was nothing, Zaylie stood frozen in the doorway. It was apparent that Gran had kept the room clean, but nothing was moved from its place. The vanity mirror was still covered in photos of Zoe and her high school friends, and NSYNC posters still hung from the walls. Several of Zoe's beautiful drawings were sitting about the room, and for a moment, Zaylie was taken back. Back to that awful night twenty years ago, when she and Zoe were sitting on her bed, drawing and laughing. Zaylie's eyes drifted over to the closet then, and she suddenly found it very hard to breathe.

"I used to hide love notes in my air vents," Rita was rambling as she hopped up on Zoe's bed and shone her phone's flashlight into the ceiling vent. With a sigh, she muttered, "Nothing there."

Rita continued to search the room while Zaylie simply stood by silently and watched. Under the bed, behind the posters on the wall, and beneath

Zoe's dresser and chest of drawers. She even took each drawer out to make certain none of them had a false bottom or something taped underneath.

"Rita, we're liable to wake Gran," Zaylie finally said in a raspy voice.

"If we haven't bothered her yet, I doubt we will now," Rita replied as she hurried over to the closet.

When Rita opened the closet doors, Zaylie stepped back, bumping her shoulder against the doorframe. Memories of that dark, horribly tight space made her skin crawl. She could still see herself, huddled in the corner, shivering and crying when her parents arrived. She'd been terrified it was *him,* coming back for her.

"Zaylie!" Rita all but screamed. "I found something!"

Shaking herself out of her dark thoughts, Zaylie took a hesitant step forward and asked, "W-what?"

Rita emerged from the closet with a tiny scrap of paper clasped in her hand. "Since there is still carpet in this room, I pulled one of the corners up against the wall in the closet," she explained in a rush of words. "I used to hide things under the carpet in my old room, too, remember? Anyway, I found this piece of paper stuffed underneath."

With trembling fingers, Zaylie took the torn scrap of paper and unfolded it. Written in Zoe's whimsy, delicate handwriting was what appeared to be an email address and password.

"This isn't Zoe's email address," Zaylie stated, her brow furrowing. "Or, at least, it's not the one she normally used."

Her eyes widening, Rita clasped Zaylie by the arm and said, "So, she had a secret email! Let's go log on to your computer."

The two hurried back down the hall and into Zaylie's room. After realizing there wasn't an intruder in the house, Smutti had gone back to bed and was curled up, fast asleep. When Zaylie and Rita entered, however, she opened one eye and looked at them with an air of annoyance.

Opening her laptop, Zaylie sat on her bed and quickly typed in the email address and password with trembling fingers. Within seconds, she was signed in, and Zoe's inbox lit up the screen. For a split second, Zaylie froze. She'd just entered a secret realm of her sister's life that no one had ever known about. It almost felt sacred, as if Zaylie was opening a thousand-year-old treasure chest.

"Look at that folder there," Rita said, breaking the silence. She was looking over Zaylie's shoulder and reached around to point to the left side of the screen.

Her eyes following Rita's finger, Zaylie clicked on a folder labeled "The two of us".

"Isn't that the name of an old NSYNC song?" Rita asked.

"I think so," Zaylie replied, her eyes widening when the folder opened to reveal hundreds of emails from a Captain Jack.

"*I can't stop thinking about you,*" Zaylie read out loud from the last email Zoe had saved. "*The picture you drew of the two of us is perfect...that's how I want us to stay, forever. I know your parents will object to us dating, but I don't want to keep sneaking around. You deserve better than that."*

"Why do you think your parents would have objected?" Rita asked when Zaylie stopped reading.

"My guess would be that he was several years older than her," Zaylie replied as she clicked on another email.

"It looks like that one is from Zoe," Rita said as she leaned closer to get a better look.

"Last night was so much fun! I loved sitting on the pier, listening to the ocean as we talked," Zaylie read. *"I love you, Captain Jack, and I can't wait to tell the world."*

Zaylie and Rita spent the next two hours going through every email from Captain Jack, but there was never anything said that could identify him. They talked about how they loved spending time together and of how important it was to keep their relationship private. There were a couple of times where they mentioned seeing each other at a party, but Zaylie still couldn't conjure up any clues.

"Who do you think this Captain Jack is?" Rita wanted to know after they'd read the last email.

Zaylie sighed and shook her head. "I wish I knew," she replied. She reached up to close her laptop, but hesitated as an idea suddenly popped into the back of her mind. Chewing on her bottom lip for a moment, she then opened the very last email Captain Jack had sent and hit "reply".

"Zaylie, you're not!" Rita gasped, jumping up on her knees. "Do you think he'll answer? Do you think he'll even get it?"

"I don't know, but I've got to try," Zaylie muttered as she began typing.

"I know who you are, Captain Jack, and I need to talk to you about my sister."

CHAPTER 24

The next morning, Zaylie printed out a few of Zoe and Captain Jack's emails and went to see Bill. When she told him of Rita's find, he was blown away.

"I can't believe we missed this all those years ago," he stated as he read through the emails.

"I guess y'all just didn't realize how teenaged girls think," Zaylie replied with a chuckle. "Any ideas on who Captain Jack is?"

"Other than Johnny Depp?" he asked. "I'm afraid not, but I can ask someone if it's possible to trace the IP address after all this time."

Nodding, Zaylie thanked him and left. She was heading to the Harper house next to see Erica but decided to grab some coffee on the way. When she stepped into the coffee shop, she was surprised to see Cameron Sterling standing in line.

"I assumed you would have someone pick up your coffee for you," Zaylie said when she stepped in line behind him.

Cameron turned to look at her in surprise. He was wearing gym clothes, and his normally perfect hair was mussed and sweaty.

"I do, but he's out sick today," he replied with a charming smile. "I actually make an amazing caramel macchiato at home; you should come by

189

sometime and have one."

Is he hitting on me? Zaylie wondered.

With a smile of her own, Zaylie asked, "If that's the case, then why are you here?"

Cameron laughed. "I decided I wanted to enjoy our quiet little island today before the July 4th crowd hits," he replied. "I'm usually either cooped up in my house or jetting from city to city for business meetings. I rarely get to just relax and do whatever I want."

"Oh, the sorrows of being rich," Zaylie replied in a half teasing, half sarcastic tone.

Laughing again, Cameron winked and said, "Yes, indeed."

The line moved forward, and Zaylie decided to take another chance at asking Cameron about Zoe.

"Did you ever have any nicknames when you were younger?" she asked.

Cameron looked at her oddly. "Uh, I suppose," he replied. "My frat used to call me Apollo."

"After the Greek god, huh?" Zaylie asked, resisting the urge to roll her eyes. "How fitting."

"I agree," he stated with a grin.

"How about Captain Jack?"

Cameron was taking a step forward, but when Zaylie asked that last question, he stumbled slightly and bumped into the man in front of him. After mumbling an apology, he turned back to Zaylie and asked in a slightly clipped tone, "What makes you ask that?"

Zaylie shrugged nonchalantly. "Just curious."

Raising one eyebrow, Cameron stated, "No, that was never my nickname."

With that being said, Cameron turned back around and the conversation was over. After he ordered his coffee, he nodded stiffly to Zaylie and left without another word. Zaylie watched as he climbed into his Lamborghini and drove away, wondering why he'd reacted so strangely to her question.

After grabbing a couple of coffees, she drove out to see Erica again.

"I'm sorry to keep popping by like this," she apologized when Erica opened the door. Holding out one of the coffee cups, she asked, "Could I maybe come in for a minute and talk to you about something?"

Taking the cup, Erica nodded and showed Zaylie into the kitchen. "I was just about to make a big pot of soup for later," she said with a sigh as she eyed the mound of ingredients on the counter, "but I'm starting to regret that decision. Anyway, what can I do for you?"

Zaylie showed Erica the printouts and explained about finding Zoe's secret email address. "Zoe mentions a specific party during Spring Break," Zaylie said. "Do you remember that party?"

Erica climbed onto a barstool and studied over the emails for a moment. "Sort of," she finally replied. "It was at the old plantation; no one was supposed to go out there, but I heard that a bunch of college guys would be there so I talked Zoe into going. I believe that was the first party we ever went to."

"Zoe says in one of their first emails that she and this Captain Jack met at that party," Zaylie told her. "Do you know who he is?"

Erica sighed and rubbed her head. "No, I'm afraid I don't remember much about that night," she replied. "I do remember that Zoe didn't want to be there and I lost track of her; I thought she went home. She must have gone off with that guy, but I never saw her with anyone. I was...well...I got a little drunk that night."

Zaylie wondered why Zoe kept going to the parties with Erica if she was so uncomfortable, but then she realized it must have been because *he* was there.

"I think he was probably at other parties, too," Zaylie pressed. "Did she ever hang out with one guy in particular?"

Pushing the printouts away, Erica stood up and walked over to the grocery bags that were on the counter. She began unloading carrots and snap beans and other fresh vegetables, and Zaylie wondered if she was going to answer her question.

"Erica?" Zaylie asked softly.

"I'm trying to remember," Erica snapped. Resting her hands on the counter, she said, "The only guy I remember her being around the most was Cameron, but that was because he wouldn't leave her alone."

Erica sounded annoyed, and Zaylie couldn't

seem to pinpoint why. She began chopping the carrots in an almost angry fashion, and her jaw was clenched tightly.

"Are you sure Cameron wasn't Captain Jack?" Zaylie asked hesitantly. "Maybe Zoe was only pretending that she wasn't interested."

Erica stopped chopping and sighed. Looking over at Zaylie, she said, "I don't know for sure, Zaylie. I'm sorry."

Zaylie nodded and stood up to gather the emails. "Thanks for your help, Erica," she said.

As Zaylie drove home, she got a phone call from the manager at her training center, Leslie.

"Hey, what's up?" Zaylie asked, hoping nothing was wrong at the center.

"We just received an email," Leslie replied, and Zaylie could hear one of the dogs barking in the background. "A young woman and her mom were hiking on the Appalachian trail, and the mom went missing over the weekend. The daughter is begging us to help."

"Okay, I'll check the emails when I get back to the house," Zaylie replied. "How is everything going there?"

"Mate is coming along nicely with his training," Leslie replied. "That other new rescue, though, isn't catching on as quickly as I'd like."

"He's still young," Zaylie said. "Give him a bit more time. Are the others coming along well?"

"Yes, especially Luna," Leslie stated, and Zaylie could hear the smile in her voice. "She makes me think a lot of Smutti."

"There aren't many dogs as amazing as Smutti, so that's wonderful news," Zaylie said. "Keep me posted. If I decide to go up to the Appalachian Trail, I may stop by for a day or so and check in on everything."

"Sounds good," Leslie replied. "See you later, boss."

Once Zaylie got home, she immediately checked the company emails. According to the daughter, Kris, she and her mother, Peg, had been hiking the trail from Georgia to the North Carolina border. On Saturday afternoon, Peg told Kris to walk on ahead and she would catch up.

"She said she wanted to go slower and take some pictures," Kris wrote in the email. *"After a couple of hours, I stopped to wait on her. When she never showed, I went back to find her but it's like she just disappeared. I read online that your dogs are the best. Please come help me find my mom. I'll pay whatever you want, just please help me. I'm sharing our GPS location, just in case you can come."*

Her heart clenching with sympathy, Zaylie immediately responded that she'd be there as soon as possible. Glancing over at the email printouts and box of case files, Zaylie closed her computer and sighed. It looked like, once again, Zoe's case would have to wait.

CHAPTER 25

Very early the next morning, Zaylie and Smutti flew into the Western Carolina Regional Airport. After renting a car, Zaylie drove out to the trailhead and parked. She then grabbed her backpack and supplies, put Smutti on a leash, and set out to meet Kris and the rest of the search party. Given the coordinates, she hoped it would only take a few hours to reach them.

The trail was rough, and Zaylie wondered why anyone would choose July to go for a hike. Even though the cover of the trees provided a bit of a reprieve from the swelteringly hot sun, the air was still very warm. By the time they reached the search party over five hours later, Zaylie was already exhausted and bathed in sweat.

After introducing herself to the law enforcement officers who were heading up the search, Zaylie was surprised to see a familiar face standing among the others.

"Samuel Banks, it's so good to see you!" Zaylie greeted the fellow SAR handler with a warm smile and hug. Samuel and his dogs were amazing, and the fact that they obviously hadn't found Peg yet worried her.

"You, too, Zaylie," Samuel replied, his ebony skin

glistening with sweat. "I'm glad you're here. My boys and I searched all day yesterday and again this morning, but they just can't find a scent."

"Thank you so much for coming, Miss Layne," Kris said, stepping forward to shake Zaylie's hand. "I'm so worried. There was a heavy rain on Sunday, and Mr. Banks thinks that's why his dogs can't find Mom's scent. Do you think your dog will be able to?"

Kris looked to be on the edge of hysteria. It was obvious she hadn't slept in days, and the fear in her eyes was haunting. Reaching out, Zaylie touched Kris on the arm and smiled encouragingly.

"We'll give it our best," she told her. "How far are we from the place where you last saw your mom?"

Kris rubbed her left shoulder and said, "I'm not entirely certain. We were about seventeen miles from the trailhead, but I don't know the exact location."

"Take me to the approximate place and we'll start from there," Zaylie said. "Do you have a piece of Peg's clothing?"

Kris nodded. "Yeah, it's in my backpack."

"Grab it and let's go," Zaylie instructed. While Kris hurried off, Zaylie looked at Samuel and asked, "Will you come with us? I'd feel better if you were there."

"My team can continue here with the boys," Samuel replied, nodding his head toward two other men and three bloodhounds. "They haven't found anything yet, but the search party is hoping

Peg came this way. If Smutti doesn't pick up anything back at point A, maybe my boys will find a scent here."

Kris returned with the backpack, and the four of them headed back down the trail. They came across a few hikers along the way, but none of them had seen Peg. As they walked, Zaylie asked questions.

"Tell me again why your mom wanted you to go on without her," she said.

"She used to be a freelance photographer," Kris replied, "so she brought her camera along with her. When she realized we were nearing the end of our hike, she said she wanted to go at a slower pace and take some pictures. I was going to stay with her, but she's always preferred to take pictures alone; it's her personal time to truly connect with the world around her. So, when she told me to go on ahead and that she'd catch up with me later that night, I didn't think much about it. But then she never showed, and I realized I'd made a horrible mistake."

Tears choked Kris's voice then, and Zaylie and Samuel exchanged a look. If Peg died, Kris would always blame herself.

"How old is your mom?" Zaylie asked.

"Fifty-two," Kris replied, sniffling.

"Is she accustomed to being out in nature and taking care of herself?"

Zaylie hated to keep prying Kris for information, but the more she knew, the more she would be able to help.

Kris sighed. "Sort of," she replied. "She has a fire starter and a bit of food in her pack, but I don't think she had much water left. She has a map and compass, but she was never very good at reading either one. She relied on me for things like that, and I...I just left her behind."

Stopping, Zaylie touched Kris on the arm and said firmly, "You've got to stop doing this to yourself. I know you're worried and completely exhausted, but I need you to focus. You know your mom better than anyone else, and that may be the only thing that will help us locate her. So, stop blaming yourself and let's find her. Okay?"

Kris stared at Zaylie, her black encircled eyes so bloodshot that Zaylie didn't know how the poor girl was still going. After a moment, she took a deep breath and nodded resolutely.

"Yes, ma'am," she said, her voice stronger than before. Squaring her shoulders, she turned and marched on down the trail.

"Good job," Samuel muttered under his breath. "For a minute there, I was afraid she was going to lose it."

"We've got to find her, Samuel," Zaylie replied. "If Peg didn't have much water, there's no way she can survive in this heat for much longer."

"I know," he replied with a sigh. "And since she obviously veered off the trail, there's not a water source within several miles."

The further they walked, the more worried

Zaylie became. This wasn't the first search and rescue operation she'd joined along the Appalachian Trail, but the fact that no scent could be found due to the heavy rains was not a good sign.

They walked for almost three hours before Kris finally stopped and said, "I think this is it."

"Are you sure?" Zaylie asked as she poured some water into Smutti's portable bowl.

"I remember there were some funny shaped rocks, like those over there," Kris replied, pointing to an area on their left. "I can't be completely sure, but I hope I'm right."

"Okay." Zaylie nodded. "After we all rest for a bit, let's see if Smutti can get a scent."

They sat down on some rocks to rehydrate and eat a bit of trail mix while Smutti laid down and cooled off. Fifteen minutes later, they got to work. Zaylie let Smutti get a scent off Peg's t-shirt, and the dog quickly began to search the immediate area. After a few moments, she branched out into a wider radius, and Zaylie's stomach sank.

"She's not finding a scent," she said, her tone heavy. "Let's go a little further down the trail."

They walked a couple of miles down the trail, and still there was nothing. With a sigh, Zaylie suggested they go back to the rocks Kris had pointed out.

Once they made it back, Zaylie stopped and looked around, deep in thought. "If your mom wanted to take some photos, perhaps she decided to climb up to higher ground where the best views are," she muttered, half to Kris and half to herself.

At Zaylie's words, Samuel pulled a map from his backpack. "There's a summit right here," he stated, pointing to the map.

"Even if she wasn't looking for the summit and simply went off trail and got lost, she would still probably search for higher ground," Zaylie said.

"Why do you think that?" Kris asked, a speck of hope coming into her weary eyes.

"There's a better possibility of cell service," Zaylie said.

"And she'd be able to see for miles," Samuel added, "which would have helped her to get her bearings."

Looking at him, Zaylie asked, "You have the satellite phone, right?" When he nodded, she said, "I know it's getting late, but we've got enough supplies to last a couple of days. What say we head to that summit?"

Kris and Samuel readily agreed, and the four of them went off trail and headed for the top of the mountain.

CHAPTER 26

After a couple of hours of hiking, it was getting too dark to see, and the group had to stop for the night. Samuel built a fire; not because they needed the heat, but to keep the bugs and wildlife away, and Zaylie opened Smutti's dog bowl to fill with her supper.

"I don't think I've ever been so tired," Kris said with a sigh as she sat down and leaned her back against a tree.

"Better eat something and try to get some rest," Zaylie told her. "Sunrise is at 6:30."

Samuel put some water over the fire to boil and pulled out three packs of freeze-dried chicken and dumplings.

"I never figured you to be a chef, Samuel," Zaylie stated teasingly.

"Just wait 'til you taste dessert," he replied with a grin. "Ice cream sandwiches."

"No way!" Zaylie laughed. "I might have to pass on that one."

While Kris dozed against the tree, Zaylie and Samuel talked about their many adventures. They'd met up on several rescue missions, and Zaylie had come to trust his instincts. He was raised in South Carolina and knew a lot about the low country, which had proven to be an amazing asset during disaster searches after hurricanes. He was a good man, and while he was only about ten years older than Zaylie, he had an old soul.

Once the food was ready, Zaylie roused Kris and the three ate their supper. Surprisingly, the ice cream sandwiches weren't that bad, and once they were finished, everyone spread out their blankets and tried to get some sleep.

As Zaylie curled up next to Smutti, she listened to the crickets chirping and the occasional rustling of the forest around them. Black bears and wild boars were common in the mountains, but she and Samuel both had guns if the fire didn't scare any potential predators away. Plus, she knew Smutti would alert them to anyone or anything in the area.

Looking up through the treetops, Zaylie could see the stars and she sighed, feeling a little downhearted. What if they couldn't find Peg? Or what if they did, and it was too late? After Lauren and Tia, Zaylie wasn't sure she could handle another death so soon. Every night, before falling asleep, she would see their faces and wonder if there was something else she could have done to save them.

Smutti raised her head and softly licked Zaylie's cheek, as if letting her master know everything was going to be okay. Giving the dog a rub behind the ears, Zaylie kissed her on the nose and closed her eyes, finally drifting off into a deep sleep.

At 6:25 the next morning, Smutti awakened Zaylie when she got up to stretch her large body like an overzealous yoga instructor. With a groan, Zaylie pushed herself off the hard ground and sat up. The sun was beginning to rise, birds were singing and flitting from tree to tree like happy little creatures, but Zaylie didn't feel so chipper. In fact, she felt like she had been trampled by a herd of wild horses.

"I'm getting way too old for this sleeping on the ground business," Samuel commented with a yawn.

"My thoughts exactly," Zaylie replied.

Kris stirred at the sound of their voices and then slowly sat up to look around with a look of confusion on her face. She looked utterly and completely exhausted, and Zaylie knew that a few hours' worth of sleep on the hard ground wasn't what she needed. After a moment, it sank in where she was, and she greeted her fellow campers in a tired voice.

While Kris walked out into the trees to relieve herself, Zaylie asked Samuel in a low voice, "No calls came in on the satellite phone, huh?"

Samuel shook his head. "No," he replied.

With a sigh, Zaylie poured some more food into Smutti's bowl and wondered where Peg could be. With the heavy rains washing away her tracks and apparently her scent, would they ever find her?

After eating a quick breakfast, the foursome headed out. They had another four miles to go before they reached the summit, and already the morning was hot and surprisingly humid for the mountains. Sunbeams pierced through the tops of the trees, and Zaylie laughed when Smutti had to force herself to stay focused when a rabbit hopped across their trail.

The crunching of leaves, birds chirping, and Samuel humming under his breath were the only sounds around as they traveled further and further away from the main trail. Zaylie kept checking her phone, wondering if they were getting any cell reception the higher they climbed. Finally, after nearly three hours of intense hiking, the trees broke and the top of the summit came into view.

"Wow," Zaylie breathed when they reached the top, and she grabbed Smutti's collar to stop her from going further.

They could see for miles. The graceful slopes of the mountains that stretched out before them was stunning, and the way the sun played along the tops of the peaks, creating shadows and soft movement, was breathtaking. Zaylie knew how beautiful the Blue Ridge Mountains were, but she never grew tired of seeing them.

After they all caught their breath, Samuel began pointing out certain landmarks and specific locations that Peg might have noticed had she been there.

"If she had a map, it would have been much easier for her to gain her bearings from up here," he said.

Squinting, Zaylie shaded her eyes and pointed to an area that was more heavily wooded than the rest.

"With the rain coming, she might have chosen a place like that to try to take shelter," Zaylie said. "And that would explain why the helicopters have been unable to spot her."

As they discussed their next plan of action, the wind softly began to shift. Suddenly, Smutti stood and sniffed the air, her ears perked up and eyes alert. Her heart catching, Zaylie motioned for the others to take notice, and they all stopped to watch the large dog. Her black coat glistened in the sunlight, and with her golden eyes and nose pointed upward, she looked just like a wolf getting ready to track its prey.

Turning away from the summit, Smutti barked sharply and took off into the woods. Zaylie quickly let out a shrill whistle, and the dog instantly stopped to wait for them to catch up.

"Has she gotten a scent?" Kris asked hopefully as they hurried after Smutti.

"Yes," Zaylie replied, her heart pounding.

When they found Smutti, Zaylie attached the bells to her collar and gave the signal for her to keep tracking. Smutti spun around and took off like lightning through the woods, and the three adults quickly followed.

They ran and ran, pushing tree limbs and bushes out of the way as they followed the sound of the bells. Every few minutes, Smutti would stop and wait for them to catch up, and then she'd start again. Sweat dripped off Zaylie's forehead and trickled slowly down her back. Her heart was pounding, and she could hear the sound of breathless panting coming from her other two companions. Would Peg still be alive, or would they be too late? What if the wind shifted again, and Smutti lost the scent? All of these thoughts ran wildly through Zaylie's mind, but she pushed them aside and prayed to find Peg safe and sound.

Finally, when Zaylie wasn't certain that any of them could continue running, Smutti's bark from just up ahead rang out through the trees and Zaylie knew she'd found her. Within seconds, they broke into a small clearing with a heavy covering of limbs and branches overhead, and Zaylie spotted Smutti standing over a large, and very still, body.

"Mom!" Kris cried, running to her mother.

Zaylie and Samuel followed and kneeled at Peg's side. Her eyes were closed, and for one heart-rending moment, Zaylie thought she was dead.

"She's still alive," Samuel said as he checked her pulse, his face breaking into a huge smile.

While Samuel made the call to the other rescuers, Zaylie checked Peg's vitals. Her pulse was very weak and her breathing shallow, but if they could get her out of there soon and into a hospital, she would make it.

Wrapping her arms around Smutti's furry neck, Zaylie whispered, "We did it, girl. We did it."

CHAPTER 27

O nce the rescuers arrived, Peg was treated by the medics and then transported out. After receiving perfuse thanks from Kris and saying their goodbyes, Zaylie, Samuel, and a few other volunteers headed out before the rest. Smutti and Samuel's dogs were tired, but they were used to this type of hard work and pushed on like troopers. It was a long and tedious journey, but they made it back to their vehicles just before nightfall.

"I think I could sleep for a week," Samuel said with a laugh as he hugged Zaylie goodbye.

"You and I both," she replied with a tired smile. "Safe travels, Samuel. It was so good to see you."

Even though Zaylie was exhausted, she decided to drive to the training center, which was only a couple of hours away. She figured it would be better to sleep there for the night and drive home tomorrow, rather than try to catch a flight home tonight.

The drive to Crescent Moon was not as easy as Zaylie would have liked. It was July the 3rd, which meant everyone was headed to Gatlinburg and Pigeon Forge for the weekend. After sitting in traffic for a bit, she finally turned off the interstate and took the back roads. By the time she made it to

Crescent Moon, the center was closed.

The night was dark and still as Zaylie turned down the long driveway that led to her family's log cabin. After her dad remarried, he'd sold the house to Zaylie, but she'd never really thought of it as "hers". Although it was a beautiful house and she had a lot of good memories there, it had never felt like a true home. Instead, it was more like a home away from home.

"Alright, girl, let's get some much needed sleep," Zaylie said to Smutti as she parked in front of the cabin.

Zaylie grabbed her overnight back, pulled her house keys from her purse, and climbed up the front porch steps. Crickets sang from the trees and bushes, and the porch swing bumped softly back and forth in the breeze. As soon as they got inside, Zaylie went to the shower while Smutti curled up in her bed and immediately went to sleep. Fifteen minutes later, Zaylie crawled into her own bed and was asleep within seconds.

The next morning, Zaylie went over to the training center to see how everything was going.

"It's so good to see you," Leslie said with a bright smile as she gave her boss a hug. Pulling back to eye her closer, she asked, "How are you holding up with everything that's happened?"

"I'm okay," Zaylie replied with a tired smile.

"Well, Tyler has everyone outside getting

warmed up," Leslie said, letting the subject drop. "Come on, let's go join them. The dogs have been missing you."

Zaylie spent a couple of hours helping train the dogs, and she realized how much she'd missed being there. Training was always a fulfilling and exhilarating experience for her, and one that she never grew tired of.

It was almost eleven when Zaylie got a text from Gran.

"Will you be home in time for the fireworks tonight?" she wanted to know.

"Yes, ma'am," Zaylie replied. *"I'll be leaving here shortly."*

Putting her phone back into her pocket, Zaylie excused herself to go inside for a moment. As she walked toward the large facility, she noticed a delivery truck pulling in.

"I'll see about it," she called to Leslie. When Smutti started to follow her, she told her to stay outside with the others.

Zaylie went into the building and hurried around to the front door. The training center was quite large, with an inside gym that was also used for training, kennels where the dogs slept, and several offices for the workers. There was also a kitchen, several bathrooms, and a shower that the handlers would use on particularly hot days.

"Sorry to keep you waiting..." Zaylie started to say as she opened the front door, but stopped mid-sentence when she realized Clark Schultz was the man on the other side.

"Hello, Miss Layne," he greeted her with a friendly smile. "I didn't realize you were here."

"Smutti and I were out on a mission not too far from here, so we stopped in for the night," she explained. "You're bringing us more supplies, I presume?"

Clark nodded and handed Zaylie a paper to sign. "Yep. This is my last stop, and then I'm heading home," he said as she signed the paper. "Will you be staying here very long?"

Zaylie returned the paper and shook her head. "No," she replied. "I'll be heading home today, too."

After Clark unloaded his truck, Zaylie showed him into the supply room. While he unloaded the boxes and stacked them in the corner, she asked him about his family.

"My dad left us when I was twelve," he replied in a gruff tone. "My mom wasn't well and couldn't support us on her own, so I started working when I was fourteen. She died when I was twenty-six."

Zaylie hadn't expected his life story when she'd asked about his family and was surprised he'd voluntarily shared so much.

"I'm sorry to hear that," she said softly. "Do you have any siblings?"

Grunting as he picked up a particularly heavy box, Clark nodded and said, "Yeah, a younger brother and sister. They both live in Savannah now."

Before Zaylie could stop herself, she blurted out,

"You never married?"

Clark looked at her in surprise, and Zaylie thought she saw his jaw clench in the dim lighting.

"No," he stated in a clipped tone.

When he turned his back on her and continued with his work, Zaylie couldn't help asking one final question.

"I know this is random, but did you ever have any nicknames?"

Clark unloaded his final box, and as he turned to push his hand truck from the room, she wondered if he was going to answer her. When he reached the doorway where she stood, he stopped and stared at her with a hard look in his deep-set blue eyes. Zaylie took a small step back, stopping when she bumped into the wall behind her. It wasn't until that very moment that she realized there was only one exit to this room, and Clark was blocking it. There was also no one inside the training center except for the two of them; everyone else had either taken the day off or was outside.

"Yes, I did have a nickname when I was young," he finally said, his deep voice echoing in the room.

Zaylie swallowed. "Oh?" she asked, her throat suddenly very dry and raspy. "What was it?"

"White Trash."

With those words, Clark walked from the room and didn't look back. Zaylie stared after him, relieved that he was leaving and also feeling guilty for asking him that last question. He'd apparently had a hard life, and she'd forced him to bring up painful memories. If all he'd ever known was pain and misery on the island, though, why had he stayed there all these years?

The front door banged shut, and within a few seconds, she could hear the roar of his truck as he drove away.

CHAPTER 28

After dropping the rental car off at the airport and picking up her own car, Zaylie made it back to Whisper Island just after seven o'clock. Everyone was already down at the pier getting ready for the fireworks, so she quickly changed her clothes and fed Smutti before joining the others.

When Zaylie found Gran at one of the local restaurants, she was surprised to see that Ryker, Rita, their dad and his girlfriend were with her. After hugging Mr. Steele, Zaylie moved to sit by Rita but paused when she realized Kaleb Bates sat on her other side.

"Kaleb," she said in surprise, "I didn't know you were coming this weekend."

Rita looked at him and beamed. "He wanted to meet my dad," she stated. "Isn't it great that he's here?"

"Marvelous." Zaylie smiled as she sat across from them.

Looking around, Rita asked, "Where's Smutti?"

"She's really tired after such an eventful trip, so I left her home," Zaylie replied.

"It's not good for dogs to be around fireworks anyway," Mr. Steele's girlfriend, Helen, spoke up in her typical abrasive voice.

"Smutti isn't like other dogs," Rita stated in an annoyed tone.

Helen sat up straighter and leaned around Mr. Steele to look at Rita adamantly. "I still think it's too risky..." she began, but before the two could engage in an all-out war, Zaylie interrupted.

"You're right, Mrs. Buchanan," she said, kicking Rita under the table when she rolled her eyes. "I wouldn't want to take any chances with her."

Nodding in satisfaction, Helen sat back and took a sip of her lemonade.

"Nice way to run interference," Ryker, who was sitting on her left, muttered. "They've been going at it all afternoon."

"Kaleb isn't doing a very good job of distracting her, huh?" Zaylie asked.

"You know Rita," he stated with a chuckle. "The ultimate multitasker."

Zaylie helped Rita eat the rest of her grilled chicken and pineapple sandwich, and then they all headed down to the beach to find a place with a good view. The sun was starting to make its descent, but the fireworks wouldn't start for almost another hour. The beach was already crowded, though, and Zaylie spotted several familiar faces gathering around. Erica was setting up a lounge chair next to some friends while Bill and Devon talked with the firefighters who would be doing the fireworks. Cameron Sterling's mansion could be seen up on the bluff, overlooking the crowd like a king's palace; Zaylie thought she could even see him sitting out on the back terrace.

"Be nice to live in a place like that, wouldn't it?" Kaleb asked, nodding toward Cameron's home.

"I don't know," she replied. "It looks kind of lonely to me."

"I guess money isn't a great replacement for people," he stated.

"No, it's not." Turning to look at him, Zaylie asked, "So, how do you like our little island?"

Kaleb stuffed his hands into his pockets and looked down as he dug his toes into the sand. "It's nice," was all he would say. Looking up again, he glanced around and asked, "Where is Rita?"

"She stopped to browse in one of the shops," Zaylie replied.

"I think I'll go find her," he muttered as he hurried away.

Zaylie sat down in one of the lounge chairs and blew out a deep breath. The last several days had taken their toll, and as soon as the fireworks were over, she planned to go home and go straight to bed. Looking around, she saw that Gran was talking with several of her friends and Helen was giving Mr. Steele an earful about something. Ryker had joined Bill and the firefighters, but Devon had seemingly disappeared.

Spotting movement underneath a palm tree to her left, Zaylie turned to look and was surprised to find Clark Schultz sitting off to himself. He was all alone, but by the expression on his face, he seemed to prefer it that way.

"Tell me again why we didn't set up our chairs on the grass like some of the others?"

Turning, Zaylie shook her head and laughed as she watched Rita tottering through the sand in her thick wedge sandals.

"Rita, why didn't you just wear flip-flops like the rest of us?" she asked.

"I hate those things," she stated, plopping down next to Zaylie. "They're so unfashionable. Hey, where's Kaleb?"

Before Zaylie could respond, her cell phone chimed, and she unlocked the screen to find that she had a new text message from an unknown number.

"It's Captain Jack," the message read. *"I have to talk to you. Meet me at Driftwood Park in ten minutes."*

Zaylie's heart kicked into overdrive, and she sat up straight. He'd gotten her email! Reaching into her purse, she grabbed her keys and started to stand up, but stopped when Rita grabbed her arm.

"Where are you going?" she wanted to know.

Zaylie showed her the text and said, "I've got to hurry. It'll take at least ten minutes to get to my car and drive over there."

"Zaylie, have you lost your mind?" Rita all but shrieked. "You can't go over to that spooky place all by yourself!"

"Then come with me, and hurry up," Zaylie said as she yanked Rita from her chair.

"Shouldn't we get the police or something?" Rita

wanted to know, grasping onto Zaylie's arm when her ankle turned and she almost face planted in the sand.

"Rita, this is the man my sister was dating," Zaylie stated. "Not the one who killed her."

"I hope you're right," Rita muttered.

Exactly eight minutes later, Zaylie pulled off the road and parked. It was almost dark outside, so she quickly grabbed a flashlight from the glove compartment. As she changed into a pair of buckle sandals, she told Rita to stay in the car.

"But what if you need my help?" Rita asked.

"I'll go ahead and type out an SOS message," she said, pulling out her phone to do just that. "If I feel threatened, I'll send it and you can come running to my rescue, okay?"

"Okay, but hurry up, will you?" Rita sighed. "I don't want to miss the fireworks. And be careful!"

Zaylie climbed from the car and hurried down the wooded path that led to the meeting place. Driftwood Park had once been a maritime forest, but after years of erosion, it became a sandy beach lined with massive, gnarly pieces of driftwood. It was a popular place for visitors, tourists, and even weddings, but it was completely deserted tonight, as everyone was over at the main beach for the fireworks.

The path ended, and Zaylie stopped for a moment to look around. When she saw no one, she slowly stepped from the cover of the trees onto the open beach. The tide was just starting to come in, and the sound of water lapping at the shore masked the sound of Zaylie's footsteps as she tentatively looked around. There was something mysterious and other-worldly about this place. The way the weathered branches that lay lifelessly on the shore reached up into the twilight sky sent chills down Zaylie's spine. It seemed that the twisted trees and limbs were reaching out to her, begging for her to turn back. The sky was streaked with dark pink and purple against a navy blue canvas, and the area steadily grew darker with each second.

"Where is he?" she thought, starting to feel nervous as she clicked on the flashlight. She checked her phone, but he hadn't texted again. Had he decided to back out?

Just then, she thought she heard a rustling in the woods behind her. She stopped and shined the light in that direction, but couldn't make anything out through the thick shrubbery.

"Captain Jack?" she called out.

Suddenly, an odd feeling swept over her, and she turned to see a dark silhouette step out from behind a large piece of driftwood. For a moment, she felt a spark of excitement that she was about to meet the man her sister had loved, but then a sense of foreboding took its place. There was something very ominous and threatening about the way the man stood there so quietly, staring at her, with his shoulders squared and tense. She moved the flashlight's beam toward him, and it was then that she realized he was wearing a baseball cap, which completely masked his features.

"Who are you?" she asked, her voice carrying on the wind.

As quickly as he'd appeared, he stepped back behind the tree and melted into the shadows. Squinting, Zaylie tried to see where he'd gone, but it was too dark. Had he changed his mind and decided not to talk to her?

Just then, she heard the sound of a song being hummed. She tilted her head and listened, trying to figure out why the tune seemed so familiar.

"Are the stars out tonight? I don't know if it's cloudy or bright. I only have eyes for you, dear."

The words flowed through her mind, but Zaylie couldn't figure out what it was about the song that made her feel so edgy. And then it hit her.

He's tall and muscular. Constantly hums "I only have eyes for you". -L

Lauren's note flashed before her eyes, and Zaylie drew in a quick breath. Suddenly, she saw his shadowy silhouette dart out from behind the tree, and she took a stumbling step backward. He was coming right toward her.

Zaylie's brain screamed at her to run, and it was in that moment she realized she'd made a mistake. Just as Rita had suspected, this wasn't the man Zoe was in love with. This was her killer.

Spinning on her heel, Zaylie ran toward the opposite end of the beach, where another path would lead her back out to the road. She darted through the graveyard of forgotten corpses, her skirt getting caught on the tips of sharp branches as she passed. She grappled for her phone, almost dropping it as she hit "send" on the SOS text. It looked as if it wasn't going to go through, and her heart sank. Apparently, there wasn't much cell service out here.

Tripping over a small piece of driftwood, Zaylie looked over her shoulder, but she couldn't see him; it had grown too dark. She stopped and turned her flashlight back on, her chest heaving as she shined it all around. The area was eerily quiet; even the ocean seemed to have stilled. Fireworks began to crack sporadically in the distance, but there was no other sound to be heard. Had he left? Or was he simply lurking behind those ancient trees, waiting to pounce on her?

Swallowing past the lump in her throat, Zaylie kept going until she finally reached the exit path. Thick trees and shrubbery lined either side of the small footpath, creating an even darker, shadowy atmosphere. The path curved around and around, leading Zaylie further and further away from the beach. Palm trees rustled overhead, and just then, she thought she heard the crunching of footsteps in the sand behind her. She turned and shined the light back down the path, but couldn't see past the bend. Thick, knobby branches reached out like fingers through the darkness as leaves and shrubs shifted and stirred in the wind.

Clutching the small flashlight like a weapon,

Zaylie picked up her pace and hurried on toward the road. It took only a few steps to realize that someone was, indeed, still following her, and she quickly broke into a run. She went as fast as she could in the soft sand, but the winding path twisted and turned so quickly that she was barely able to keep track of where she was going. The footsteps were drawing closer, and then she heard the sound of heavy breathing. She glanced over her shoulder just as a large hand reached out through the darkness and grabbed her roughly by the arm.

CHAPTER 29

With a scream, Zaylie jerked away and caught her foot on a protruding root. Her arms flailing, she stumbled and hit the ground with a painful *oomph!* Before she could catch her breath, he was upon her and his hands were wrapping around her throat.

It was too dark to see his face, and he blocked her attempts to knock the baseball cap from his head. She struggled and tried to kick and squirm from beneath him, but he was too strong for her. His hands were squeezing the life out of her, and the only thought whirling through her mind was that she'd never know who Zoe's killer was.

Suddenly, a shriek that could rival that of a screech owl sounded from behind. A light shined in Zaylie's eyes just as something hissed through the air and struck her assailant on the head with a *thud*. He jerked to the side, and with a grunt, slumped to the ground several feet away, holding his head as he moaned. Zaylie slowly sat up, dazed and confused as she stared silently at his dark figure.

"Zaylie, good grief, get up!"

Rita's long fingernails felt like an eagle's claws as she grabbed Zaylie's arm and yanked her off the ground. Before either of them could move, the man jumped to his feet. The two women gasped and stumbled back as he turned and ran down the path toward the road.

"D-did you see his face?" Zaylie asked in a breathless tone.

"No, his back was toward me," Rita said. "I wasn't exactly focused on that, anyway. I was more focused on saving your life. Are you okay?"

"I have to know who he is," Zaylie said, struggling against her friend as she tried to run after him. She knew she wasn't thinking clearly, but she needed to know who her sister's killer was.

"If you try to run that man down, I'm going to kill you myself," Rita hissed as she clutched Zaylie's arm even tighter.

They turned around and took the long way back to Zaylie's car. The return trip was nerve-wracking, to say the least. Both women half expected the man to jump out at them any second. By the time they made it back to the road, Zaylie was shaking all over. The adrenaline that had surged so strongly through her body only moments ago was now leaving her drained and trembling. Rita took over and jumped into the driver's seat, taking off down the road with screeching tires and a wild look in her eyes.

"So, now that we're out of danger for the moment, what exactly happened back there?" she wanted to know.

"You were right, Rita," Zaylie said as she reached up to touch her throat. "It wasn't Captain Jack; it was Zoe's killer."

"How many times are you going to bump into this guy before he kills *you?*" Rita asked. "Which he would have done, had I not insisted I come along. Zaylie, only cats have nine lives. You can't keep playing around with this guy."

"I was **this** close!" Zaylie cried, holding up her hands. "I could have seen his face if only you'd let me go after him."

Rita rolled her eyes. "Oh, yeah, you could have seen his face just before he killed us both," she stated drolly. "Are you going to tell the police?"

"There's no need," Zaylie replied. "He's long gone by now." With a moan, she crossed her arms and added, "I can't believe I fell for the whole Captain Jack ruse."

"You know, Zaylie, Zoe's killer and Captain Jack could be one and the same," Rita pointed out.

Zaylie shook her head stubbornly. "There's no way my sister was in love with a killer."

Glancing over at her, Rita said, "She was a kid, Zaylie. Do you know how many stories I've read about young girls falling for older guys who turned out to be psychopaths?"

Zaylie sat back against her seat and sighed. As they pulled into the parking lot a few moments later and parked, she looked at Rita and asked, "Hey, what did you throw at him, anyway?"

Rita flipped a strand of black hair over her shoulder and said saucily, "One of my shoes. Aren't you glad now that I didn't wear flip-flops?"

Zaylie and Rita made it back to the main beach just in time to catch the grand finale show. When they joined the others, Zaylie quickly looked around and took an inventory of the people on the beach. Bill was helping with the fireworks and Erica was sitting with her friends, but Devon was still nowhere to be seen. Clark had also disappeared, and when she turned to look up at Cameron's mansion, she thought she could still see his silhouette sitting out on the balcony.

As her eyes continued to scan the crowd, her gaze suddenly collided with Micah's. He'd been watching her, apparently, and when their eyes met, he smiled and waved. He was sitting with his parents, older sister, brother-in-law, and niece, and Zaylie had to admit that he looked very handsome in his jeans and button-down Hawaiian shirt. She smiled and waved in return, both to him and his mom when Mrs. Pierce spotted her.

"I still think you should tell Bill," Rita whispered, interrupting her thoughts.

"So he can yell at me again?" Zaylie asked, pulling her gaze away from Micah. "No, thanks."

The fireworks ended then, and the beach erupted in clapping, whistles, and cheering. Just when Gran and Ryker were turning to ask where Zaylie and Rita had disappeared to, Kaleb showed up.

"There you are," he said when he saw Rita. "I

think I walked through every shop looking for you."

"Oh, Kaleb, I'm sorry!" she cried, grabbing his arm as she gave Zaylie the side eye. "Zaylie and I had, uh, something we had to do. Did you miss the whole show?"

As the couple walked to Kaleb's car, Ryker stepped up next to Zaylie and said, "Dare I ask what the two of you were up to?"

"Whatever do you mean?" Zaylie asked innocently.

"The whole wide-eyed innocent thing doesn't work with me," he replied wryly. "Better leave the acting to Rita."

Zaylie's lips pursed with annoyance. "Don't you have someone to go flirt with?" she asked, raising an impatient eyebrow at him.

A slow, mischievous grin spread across his face and he asked, "Is that an invitation?"

Rolling her eyes, Zaylie started to respond but was immediately distracted when she spotted Clark and Erica standing beneath a nearby palm tree. They were discussing something in a rather intent manner, and Clark didn't look very pleased. After a moment, Devon appeared on the scene, and the conversation was over.

"You ready to go, honey?"

Turning to look at Gran, Zaylie nodded and followed the others off the beach. As they walked, she looked up once more to find that Cameron's dark figure still sat on the balcony, unmoving. It looked as if he was facing them, and she could almost feel those icy blue eyes staring down at her.

CHAPTER 30

The next morning, Zaylie got a call from Bill. At first, she was afraid he'd somehow found out about her meeting with Captain Jack, and she answered the phone with a bit of apprehension.

"Hey, Zaylie," he greeted her, and she immediately relaxed at the genteel tone in his voice. "I wanted to let you know what I found out about any other murders that took place over the last few years on June the 18th."

Zaylie's heart quickened. "What did you find out?" she wanted to know.

"I wasn't able to find anything," he replied. "If the man who killed your sister is the same man who kidnapped and killed Lauren, he hasn't murdered anyone else on June the 18th. Unless, that is, the murders weren't reported."

"Why wouldn't they have been reported?" Zaylie asked.

"Maybe the bodies were never found, or perhaps he killed women who didn't have any family," he stated. "I'm sorry I couldn't find more, Zaylie."

Zaylie thanked him and then ended the call. She sat in her room and stared out the window for awhile, deep in thought. There had to be someone on the island that remembered something. Did Zoe have any other friends? Zaylie couldn't remember, but then an idea struck her and she hurried from her own room and into Zoe's.

Once in Zoe's room, she went over to the bookcase and grabbed the last high school yearbook Zoe had received. Inside the front and back pages were dozens of handwritten notes and signatures, and Zaylie spent the next hour trying to figure out who was who. Some of the names she didn't recognize, so she looked them up on social media. Some she found, and others she didn't. Finally, one name on the very back page stood out to her, and she realized that Joan Peavey, who was now Joan Richards, was the owner of the coffee shop. According to the note she'd left in Zoe's yearbook, the two had been fairly good friends.

After putting the yearbook back, Zaylie quickly changed her clothes and went downstairs. Ryker wasn't working today, Gran was at her Saturday afternoon Bingo club, and Rita was out with Kaleb. Zaylie quickly fed Smutti, grabbed her keys, and headed out.

There were still quite a few tourists on the island for the weekend, and so it took a bit longer than usual to drive to the coffee shop. Once she arrived, she moaned in frustration. Every parking space was taken, and she had to parallel park two blocks away. When she walked inside the shop, there was a line all the way to the door.

After standing in line for several minutes, a voice said from behind, "Looks like the locals are going to have to open their own exclusive spot for coffee and pastries."

Turning to look at Micah, Zaylie smiled and said, "I agree. Any ideas on who should run it?"

"Well, since you're going to move back here and open another training center, why not throw in a coffee shop while you're at it?"

Zaylie laughed. "I don't remember saying I was going to move back here "

Micah's eyes were warm as he said, "Not yet, but I know you want to."

Zaylie raised an unconvinced eyebrow. "And just how do you know that?" she asked.

"Because I know you so well," he replied. "And you're like me; neither one of us can stay away from this place forever."

When Zaylie spotted Joan going into the supply room, she excused herself, feeling thankful for the interruption. How could Micah say he knew her so well after all these years? She'd changed; they both had. But perhaps their mutual love for the island was something that would always stay the same.

"Joan?" she asked as she gingerly stepped into the doorway of the supply room.

Joan turned to looked at her in surprise, and then she smiled as recognition lit her face. "Oh, hey," she replied. "Zaylie, right? I haven't seen you in a while. You don't visit as often as you should."

"You're right," she replied with a small laugh. "I work too much, which is something I think you can probably relate to."

Joan laughed in return. "You've got me there," she said. "Is there something I can do for you?"

"I hope so," Zaylie replied. "I was going through my sister's yearbook, and I noticed that the two of you seemed to be friends. You wouldn't happen to remember her ever mentioning a boyfriend, would you?"

Joan stopped what she was doing and rubbed her forehead as she considered the question. "She was a year younger than me, you know, so we weren't around each other too much," she replied. "I do remember seeing her at a few parties, though, which is where we sort of became friends. The whole party scene was never really our thing, so we would sit and talk sometimes. I don't remember her ever saying anything about a guy that she liked, but I have some old pictures up in the attic that you could go through. Maybe you'll come across something there."

Zaylie's eyes widened hopefully. "That would be amazing!" she exclaimed. "When could I come by?"

Joan checked her watch and said, "I won't get home until super late tonight, and then I'll need to find them for you. How about tomorrow evening around six?"

Zaylie readily agreed and thanked Joan profusely. As she left the coffee shop, she waved goodbye to Micah but didn't stop to continue their conversation. She wasn't sure how she was feeling about being around him so much, nor about his claim to still know her so well. Was there still a spark between them? She wasn't sure, nor did she want to think about that right now.

As Zaylie was walking to her car, she spotted Mr. Winters heading across the parking lot toward the coffee shop. Mr. Winters used to run the only jewelry store in town, and seeing him sparked an idea in Zaylie's mind.

"Mr. Winters, do you have a minute?" she asked the elderly gentleman who happened to be a good friend of Gran's.

His faded blue eyes wrinkled around the edges as he smiled at Zaylie. "I have more than one," he replied. "What can I do for you, Miss Layne?"

"You don't happen to still have any of your old records from the store, do you?" Zaylie asked.

Mr. Winters tilted his head to one side. "How old are we talking?"

"Twenty years," Zaylie replied a bit sheepishly. She knew it was a long shot, but she at least had to try.

"Luckily for you, I'm old school and never throw anything away," he replied with a chuckle. "I have about thirty years worth of records sitting in my garage. Was there something in particular you wanted me to find for you?"

Zaylie could hardly believe her ears. "Would you mind terribly if I asked you to look through your records between the months of May and June for a custom order twenty years ago?" she asked. "It would have been for a heart charm with initials engraved on it."

Mr. Winters patted her on the arm and nodded. "It would be my pleasure."

That evening, Mr. Steele invited everyone over to his house for a grill-out. Gran and Zaylie brought homemade potato salad and banana pudding and met everyone there at five o'clock. Rita was already there with Kaleb, and Zaylie was glad to see that Helen Buchanan wasn't among the small crowd.

"She had plans with her own kids, thank goodness," Rita told her with a satisfied smile.

"You're awful," Zaylie said with a laugh. Nodding towards Kaleb, who stood at the grill talking with Mr. Steele, she asked, "Are the two of them hitting it off?"

Rita sighed. "I think Dad feels by Kaleb the way I feel about Helen," she replied. "He doesn't seem to like him very much."

"Why not?" Zaylie asked as she grabbed a potato chip from the bowl on the patio table.

"Well, Kaleb is kind of shy," Rita said, "and Dad just keeps taking it the wrong way."

"I need a for instance," Zaylie stated.

Rita crossed her arms and said, "Okay. For instance, when Dad asked Kaleb what he does for a living, Kaleb didn't seem to want to answer him."

Zaylie's brow furrowed. "Why not?"

"He wasn't being difficult," Rita hurriedly said, rushing to Kaleb's defense. "He's just a little awkward and nervous about trying to impress

Dad."

"Well, did he ever answer him?"

Rita nodded. "Yes," she replied a bit too passively.

Zaylie eyed her friend. "What did he say?"

Rita looked down at her fingernails and cleared her throat. "He, uh, said that he's an engineer."

Zaylie frowned. "I thought he was a technician?"

Rita waved her hand in the air and said, "They're basically the same thing."

Without waiting for Zaylie to comment further, Rita hurried off to join her dad and Kaleb at the grill. Zaylie watched them for a moment, wondering why Kaleb had felt the need to embellish his career with Rita's dad but not with Rita. Was it possible he was hiding something?

Kaleb turned to look at her just then, and when Zaylie gave him a small wave, he simply stared at her for a moment before turning back around. Had he somehow sensed what she was thinking? Zaylie shivered and rubbed her arms, wondering at the sudden chill that had swept over her. Kaleb had saved her life, so why was she feeling suspicious about him? Was it simply because he was dating her best friend and she was naturally being protective?

"Penny for your thoughts," Ryker said when he stepped up beside her.

Taking the glass of sweet tea he offered her, Zaylie tilted her head and asked, "Did you ever check him out?"

"Kaleb? I sure did."

Zaylie raised her eyebrows and asked, "Well? What did you find out?"

"He's who he says he is," he replied, shrugging. "Other than a few speeding tickets, his record is clean."

"Do you like him?" she wanted to know.

Ryker sipped his tea for a moment, his eyes studying Kaleb over the rim of his glass. "He's alright," was all he would say when he lowered his glass. Looking down at her, he asked in a sarcastic tone, "Why? Don't you like him? He is, after all, supposedly a hero. According to you, that is."

"Supposedly so are you, but that doesn't mean I have to like either of you," she told him with a smirk.

Laughing, Ryker asked, "Are you still in denial about your feelings for me?"

Zaylie wrinkled her nose. "No," she replied, shaking her head. "I still know that I don't like you."

Grinning, Ryker leaned closer and said in a low tone, "That just means I'll have to work even harder to change your mind."

Zaylie couldn't help smiling as Ryker sauntered away. His cocky, flirtatious manner was a lot to deal with at times, but she was starting to feel that deep down, he had a good heart.

CHAPTER 31

The next morning, Zaylie got up early and went for a run on the beach. Even though it was early July and the heat index would most likely be well over 100 degrees, there was always a nice breeze on the beach which helped the heat to be more tolerable. Also, watching the sun rise over the ocean made it all worth it.

Once she'd finished running, Zaylie stopped and took her shoes off. She loved the feeling of the wet sand between her toes as the cool water rushed over her feet. For a moment, she closed her eyes and simply soaked it all in. The sound of the waves rushing onto the sandy shore as seagulls chirped overhead bathed her in a sense of peace. The soft breeze blew over her skin like a curtain of silk and ruffled the strands of hair around her neck which had fallen from her ponytail. She loved it here. The ocean, the island, the people...it was all a part of her. Maybe Micah was right and she *should* move back and open a second training center. Leslie was more than capable of running the center in Crescent Moon, and the business had grown enough that they could easily handle a second location. It was something to think about, and Zaylie planned to discuss it with her dad soon.

Glancing at her smartwatch, Zaylie realized she

needed to hurry if she didn't want to be late for church. With one final look at the beautiful, peaceful beachfront, she hurried up to the house and took a shower. When she came back downstairs thirty minutes later with her wet hair wrapped in a towel, Gran was standing at the stove, frying some bacon and eggs.

"Did you go for a run this morning?" she asked.

Zaylie nodded. "It was so nice," she stated with a sigh as she fixed herself a cup of coffee.

"I saw you waving at Micah Pierce and his mom Friday night," Gran said, apparently trying to keep her tone relaxed and nonchalant as she eyed Zaylie out of the corner of her eye. "Have the two of you been talking very much?"

"No, not really," was all Zaylie said. She tried not to smile as she sipped her coffee; she knew it was killing Gran to be so passive.

"He isn't as handsome as Ryker," Gran said, glancing over at Zaylie with an innocent smile. "Don't you agree?"

Zaylie had to force herself not to roll her eyes. "I think they're both nice looking men in their own way," she replied with a smile of her own.

Pursing her lips in annoyance, Gran turned back around and began flipping the bacon over with stiff, jerky movements. Zaylie shook her head and sighed softly. She knew Gran didn't want her to get back with Micah; she remembered all too well how devastated Zaylie had been when they broke up. Why she was pushing Ryker, though, she didn't know, but Gran was always trying to set her up with someone.

Before Zaylie could once again assure her grandmother that she had no intentions of dating Micah again, Rita came stumbling into the room.

"Whoa," Zaylie said, eyeing her disheveled friend with raised eyebrows. "Rough night?"

Rita plopped down next to Zaylie and nodded. Lime green gel masks lined her under eye area, her hair was piled on top of her head in an extremely messy bun, and her oversized robe hung half off of her body. She grabbed Zaylie's coffee and took a long gulp.

"After the grill-out at Dad's, Kaleb and I drove into Savannah," she said, covering a huge yawn. "Then he decided he wanted to go to Tybee Island, and it was still packed with tourists so it took ages to get off the island. We didn't get home until after one o'clock. Y'all didn't hear me come in?"

Gran nodded, and Zaylie shook her head. "I heard you, but I wasn't asleep anyway," Gran said. "I was right in the middle of a good book, and I just couldn't put it down."

"Why did Kaleb want to go to Tybee when we have a perfectly good beach here?" Zaylie wanted to know.

Rita shrugged. "Who knows? Maybe he just wanted to get away from Whisper for a bit."

"Do you know very much about this man, honey?" Gran asked as she dipped up the bacon and eggs.

"I know he saved Zaylie's life," Rita replied, smiling at her friend. "Isn't that enough?"

"Just because he helped save someone's life doesn't automatically make him a good person," Gran stated matter-of-factly.

"Gran, how could you say that?" Rita asked, her eyes widening. "If not for Kaleb, Zaylie might not be alive today!"

Before Rita managed to get even more dramatic, Zaylie quickly asked, "Has he said anything about his brother, Barley?"

Her mouth still open in preparation to continue defending Kaleb, Rita turned to look at Zaylie and blinked. "That's his youngest brother, right?" she asked, shifting uncomfortably. "He, uh, doesn't say much about him."

Zaylie's eyes narrowed. "So, you've asked about him and Kaleb won't tell you anything?"

Rita took a sip of orange juice and nodded slightly. "I think they must not get along or something. When I asked about him, Kaleb changed the subject."

"Did I mention that Barley was at my motel in West Virginia?" Zaylie asked, getting up to fix herself a piece of toast. "He was in the lobby, arguing with the lady who works there; he almost knocked me over when he stormed out. I saw him a few minutes later, standing outside underneath a tree. Something about him gave me the creeps."

"So, you're saying I shouldn't see Kaleb because he has a weird brother?" Rita asked in irritation.

Zaylie held up her hands in surrender and said, "No, I'm just saying be careful. Don't fall head over heels like you do with every guy you meet until you get to know him a little better."

Rita huffed. "I do not fall for every guy I meet," she stated indignantly.

Gran snickered and then pulled her newspaper above eye level when Rita gave her a dirty look.

With a sigh, Zaylie patted Rita's arm and said gently, "Just don't get hurt, okay?"

"Fine," Rita grumbled, stuffing her mouth with an entire piece of bacon.

The conversation soon turned to local gossip as Gran read the newspaper out loud, and then the three got ready for church. Rita, per usual, wore a full, flowy dress with the brightest colors she could find, while Zaylie wore a pastel green blouse that brought out the lighter shade of green in her eyes. Pastor Hickman preached on freedom, and he brought in a few fascinating stories about the Revolutionary War that Zaylie had never heard before. After the service, everyone stayed around to visit for a while, and then Zaylie and Gran went out to eat.

"Look who's here," Zaylie said, nodding to Mr. and Mrs. Pierce, who sat at a table nearby.

Her lip curling slightly, Gran muttered, "I suppose their son is here with them."

"Zaylie, Mrs. Ferguson, how nice to see you both again so soon!"

Trying to hide the humor in her eyes over the

expression on Gran's face, Zaylie turned to smile at Micah.

"Hi, Micah," she greeted him. "Are you just getting here?"

Micah nodded as he sat in the seat next to Zaylie, and Gran cleared her throat disapprovingly.

"Yes, I'll join my parents in a minute," he replied. "I just wanted to compliment you both on how lovely you look today."

Gran's half smile was obviously forced, but Zaylie politely thanked him. She waved to his parents, who were looking their way. They came over to chat for a few moments, and then went back to their table when the server brought their drinks.

"I guess I'd better join them now," Micah said, standing. With a warm smile, he added, "Mrs. Ferguson, I've been telling your granddaughter that she needs to move back to the island and open a second training center. Maybe you'll do a better job at convincing her."

At Micah's words, Gran perked up. When he left their table to join his parents, she looked at Zaylie and exclaimed, "My goodness, what a nice man he is!"

Zaylie's eyebrows shot up. "Are you by any chance referring to Micah Pierce, the man you've so desperately been trying to keep me away from lately?"

Gran waved a hand in the air. "Oh, I don't know what you're talking about," she sputtered. "I think his idea of your moving back to the island is marvelous! Don't you agree?"

Zaylie shook her head and smiled. "We'll see."

The server arrived then to take their order, and the conversation was interrupted. As Gran listed what she wanted to eat and gave strict instructions on how it should be cooked, Zaylie noticed a familiar face sitting among the crowd. It was Cameron Sterling, and he was seated in the corner across from a beautiful young woman. Zaylie was surprised to see him out at a restaurant that wasn't considered "exclusive". It was apparent, though, that they wanted to maintain their privacy by the way an indoor tree almost completely separated them from everyone else. The two were involved in what appeared to be a very serious conversation, and when the woman turned her head, Zaylie could see a very large bruise on her neck.

CHAPTER 32

As Zaylie drove over to Joan Richards' house later that evening, her cell phone rang. When she answered, her heart caught when Mr. Winters identified himself.

"I looked through my records, and I believe I found what you were looking for," he said.

"You did?" Zaylie asked, barely able to believe her good luck.

"Yes, ma'am," he replied, and she could hear papers rustling in the background. "The order was for a silver heart charm with the initials C.S. + Z.L. engraved on it."

Zaylie blinked. Cameron Sterling + Zoe Layne. *He* was Zoe's secret boyfriend? But Erica had said Zoe didn't like him. Was all of that, including the slap, an act to keep their relationship undercover?

"Thank you so much, Mr. Winters," Zaylie said.

Ten minutes later, she stood on Joan Richards' doorstep. She rang the doorbell and waited nervously, her mind whirling. Would she be able to find a picture of Zoe and Cameron? If so, she intended to confront Cameron with it and perhaps force some answers out of him.

"Hi, Zaylie," Joan greeted her as soon as the front door swung open. "Come on in."

Joan led her into the living room where a box

filled with photos rested on the coffee table. Zaylie could hear the sound of children's voices coming from upstairs, and she spotted a mound of toys pushed into a corner.

"I wanted to be a photographer when I was in high school, so there are a lot of pictures to go through," Joan said, laughing apologetically as she pointed to the box. "Take all the time you need, and if the kids come down and start to bother you, just holler. I'll be in the kitchen."

Zaylie nodded and sat down on the sofa. Joan was right; there were hundreds of pictures to sort through. Taking a deep breath, she made herself comfortable and got started. As she looked through each photo, she was transported back twenty years. The clothes, the hairstyles, and even the make-up and jewelry spoke of a different era. The kids were all smiling and laughing, either at inside jokes or just from sheer happiness. Each one had their own paths to choose and decisions to make that would affect the rest of their lives, but at such a young age, no one ever realizes how truly important those decisions are or what they'll mean down the road.

When Zaylie finally came across a picture with Zoe, her heart caught. She stared at her sister's beautiful smile and her eyes filled with tears. How could anyone have hurt her? She was so kind and caring, and she'd had so much potential, but her life was snatched from her at much too young of an age. It was so unfair.

After an hour of looking through nearly every photo, Zaylie was starting to get a crick in her neck. She got up and walked around for a moment, wondering if this was hopeless. So far, she'd only seen Zoe in a handful of pictures, and there was no sign of a boyfriend in any of them. Joan came in and asked if Zaylie wanted anything to drink, but Zaylie declined. After a few moments, she sat back down and reached into the box for the last stack of pictures.

Halfway through, Zaylie realized this particular stack was from a party. She slowed down and took a closer look at each photo. She spotted Cameron Sterling in several of the pictures and realized this must have been one of the parties held at his house. She saw Erica out on the dance floor with a drink in her hand, but there was no sign of Zoe.

Then Zaylie found it. The picture she'd been looking for. She stopped and stared at the photo, her heart nearly stopping. The picture was of another, unfamiliar couple, but Zoe could clearly be seen in the background. She was standing out on the balcony with her arms around a young man's neck, and they were smiling at each other. Zaylie brought the picture closer to her face and studied his features, her eyes widening with shock when she realized that it wasn't Cameron Sterling at all. It was Clark Schultz.

Quickly, Zaylie gathered up all the pictures and put them back into the box. She tucked the photo of Zoe and Clark into her purse and rushed from the room, her hands shaking. She'd finally found something concrete, and she could hardly wait to call Bill.

"I'm leaving now, Joan," she called out. "Thanks so much!"

She could hear Joan asking if she'd found anything, but she didn't stop to respond. She was too focused on getting to her car and telling Bill what she'd found.

It was well after seven, and the sun was starting to go down. As Zaylie backed out of Joan's driveway, she dialed Bill's number. When he answered, his voice sounded distorted.

"Zaylie, I'm out on the river...hardly no service. What's up?"

"I found something, Uncle Bill," she said, excitement rushing through her veins. "Can you come over to the house immediately?"

"I...barely hear you," he said, the connection cutting in and out. "I'll...there soon as I can."

The call disconnected, and Zaylie sighed. She could hardly wait to tell Bill everything she'd discovered, but it appeared she had no other choice but to wait.

Suddenly, Zaylie's phone began to screech, alerting her that the alarm system at the house had been triggered. Seconds later, Devon was calling.

"What's going on, Zaylie?" he immediately asked.

"I don't know," she replied, her heart pounding.

"I'm not home; I'm about ten minutes away."

"I'll meet you there," he said.

Zaylie tried to call both Gran and Rita, but neither answered. She then remembered that Gran was at a Sunday School class party, and Rita was out with Kaleb.

It was getting dark when she reached their property. Devon was parked at the gate, waiting for her, and Zaylie waved to him as she opened the gate and drove through. He followed her, and when she pulled up in front of the house, she could hear the security system alarming inside.

"No one is home?" Devon asked as he climbed from his truck.

Zaylie shook her head. "No, just Smutti."

Devon followed Zaylie into the house and waited as she disarmed the system. She could hear Smutti barking upstairs, but she stopped as soon as the piercing alarm quieted.

"Do you think someone is in the house?" Zaylie whispered.

The house had become eerily silent, and she glanced around uncertainly.

"Before you left earlier, did you set the system on "stay" or "away"?" Devon asked.

"Away," Zaylie replied, and then it hit her. Smutti must have come downstairs and triggered the motion detector.

"I'm so sorry, Devon," she told him, laughing sheepishly. "Next time, I'll make sure Smutti is locked inside one of the rooms."

"It's no problem," he told her graciously. "I'm just glad everything is okay."

"Well, I don't want your trip out here to be an entire waste," she said. "Why don't you come into the kitchen and I'll pack up some of Gran's homemade oatmeal cookies for you? She made them yesterday."

Devon's eyes lit up, and he nodded. "You don't have to ask me twice," he said with a chuckle.

Devon followed her into the kitchen, and as she grabbed the cookie jar from the pantry, Zaylie asked him about his son.

"Erica said he just started college," she stated. "I'm sure y'all must miss him."

Devon didn't immediately respond, and Zaylie glanced over her shoulder at him. His jaw had grown tight, and it seemed that his expression had hardened.

"Yes, we do," he finally replied, his tone a bit tense.

Zaylie's brow furrowed in confusion. Had she said something to upset him?

Just then, the kitchen door swung open. Turning in surprise, Zaylie saw that it was only Smutti, and she sighed with relief. Why was she feeling so on edge?

"Hey, girl," Zaylie greeted the dog.

Smutti moved toward her owner but then stopped and looked at Devon, her ears going back as she sniffed the air in his direction. Then, before Zaylie could comprehend what was happening,

Smutti began barking ferociously and lunged at Devon with her teeth bared.

"Smutti, stop!" Zaylie cried.

Smutti obeyed her master, but she slowly positioned herself to stand between Zaylie and Devon, her body stiff and tense as she continued to growl. Zaylie's heart was pounding as she looked up at Devon, her eyes wide.

"Devon, I'm so sorry," she apologized. "I have no idea why she…"

And then it hit her. Smutti had never been around Devon before, so why would she feel threatened by his scent unless it was one she recognized?

As if reading her mind, Devon's eyes went cold and a slow sneer spread across his face. "I knew I should have stayed away from that dog," he said, and the particular tone of voice he used sounded all too familiar.

Smutti recognized Devon's scent as the man who kidnapped Lauren and almost killed Zaylie in that West Virginia cabin.

CHAPTER 33

Zaylie stared at Devon in horror as he pulled a gun from beneath his shirt and pointed it at Smutti.

"Lock her there in the pantry or she's dead," he said to Zaylie in a steely tone.

Zaylie quickly did as he said, thankful he hadn't shot Smutti instead. Moving away from the pantry door, she went to stand by the sink so that the island separated them. Looking at Devon, her entire body was shaking as she asked in a hoarse whisper, "So…it was you? *You* killed my sister?"

"It was an accident," Devon snapped. He dropped the gun down by his side and slowly began to walk around the kitchen. "I never intended to kill her," he muttered, glancing out one of the back windows before closing the blinds.

"Then why did you?" Zaylie ground out.

Spinning around to face her, he spat out angrily, "It was her fault! If she hadn't fought me, I never would have gotten so rough with her."

Zaylie felt sick to her stomach. "So, what?" she whispered as tears filled her eyes. "You just wanted to have your fun with her and that was supposed to be the end of it? Do you really expect me to believe that? You would have gone to prison, Devon!"

"I'm telling you, it was an accident," he insisted, his face growing red. "She was still alive when I dumped her off at the park."

"What did you do?" she asked, reaching back to grip the counter for support. "I want to know. I deserve to know, Devon."

Devon shook his head and sighed. He didn't answer for a moment, and Zaylie feared that he would just shoot her with no explanation at all. She had to know what happened that night; it was all she'd lived and breathed the last twenty years.

"I was at Cameron's that night," he began in a low voice. "We had been drinking for awhile when we started talking about Zoe. He knew I had it bad for her; that's why he constantly made a play for her because that's just the kind of guy he was."

Devon leaned back against the kitchen table and crossed his arms, the gun still clutched tightly in his hands. He had a dead, faraway look in his eyes as he remembered the details of that night, and Zaylie hung on to every word.

"I'd seen the charm that Schultz had given her," he continued in a bitter, disgusted tone, "and I wanted to kill him for it. Why would she choose him over me anyway? He was a loser from the wrong side of the tracks, and she fell for *him*. I was angry, and Cameron dared me to do something about it."

Zaylie's eyes narrowed. "So, it was Cameron's idea?" she wanted to know.

Devon shrugged. "Sort of, I guess," he replied.

"We, uh, had mixed a new drug with our drinks, so we barely knew what we were saying. He went with me that night; he was out in the car while I went inside. We took her back to his place, but Cam passed out shortly after we arrived. He never knew what happened until that jogger found her body."

"You're the one who raped her then," Zaylie stated, hate surging through her body. She wanted to kill him with her bare hands; she wanted him to suffer as Zoe had suffered.

"Yeah," he replied, and something akin to guilt filled his eyes. "I remember putting my hands around her throat at one point, and I guess I went too far. She passed out, and that's when I realized what I'd done. I took her out to the park, but she wasn't dead when I left her there. I swear, Zaylie."

"Is that supposed to make me feel better?" she asked as tears coursed down her cheeks. "She laid out there and suffered until she died, Devon! How could you just leave her like that?"

His face turning blood red at Zaylie's accusations, he stood up to point the gun at her. "Shut up," he ground out. "I didn't kill her. I *didn't*."

Zaylie shook her head in disgust. "But you killed Lauren and Tia," she stated. "Why? Why did you wait twenty years to do it again?"

Devon began to laugh then, and Zaylie felt the hair on her neck stand on end. "That's the funny part," he said, still laughing. "After Zoe died, I tried to forget what happened. I started dating Erica, and when she got pregnant, I married her like any decent man should. But do you know what I found out a few months ago? He's not mine. The kid isn't even mine, and my wife has been cheating on me for years."

He continued to laugh, the maniacal sound filling the kitchen and reverberating off the walls. Smutti began to growl again, and Zaylie's eyes darted around as she searched for an available weapon. He was losing it, and she knew she didn't have much time left.

"So, you lost control and decided you needed to kill again?" she asked, hoping to keep him talking.

"Something like that," he stated, the laughter dying down as he stared at her. "You had to put your nose where it didn't belong, though, and messed everything up. It's your fault Tia died, you know. She was just a distraction, someone I could go see on the weekends, but then she started pressuring me to marry her. So, instead of breaking things off, I decided to turn it into a little game. It ended up being much more fun."

"And Lauren? I suppose that was my fault, too?"

Devon snickered. "I met Lauren on one of those dating apps," he replied. "She looked so much like Zoe, I just couldn't resist getting to know her. When she told me she was going on a camping trip with her family, I thought it would be a great opportunity to get to know her better." His eyes darkened then, and he added with a snarl, "She decided she didn't like me, though, when she realized I was much older than my picture. So, one thing led to another, and…well, you know the rest."

"How could you do this, Devon?" Zaylie asked incredulously. "How could you kill three helpless young women?"

"Four," he replied with a smirk as he aimed the gun at her head. "I knew I would have to kill you, eventually."

Suddenly, the kitchen door burst open and Bill appeared in the doorway, his gun drawn. Zaylie dove onto the floor and covered her head as Bill yelled at Devon to drop the gun. The sound of gunshots split the air then, and Zaylie screamed, squeezing her eyes shut.

As quickly as all the mayhem began, it stopped. The kitchen became deathly quiet, and the only sound Zaylie could hear was the pounding of her heart and Smutti's panicked barks from the pantry. She slowly raised her head to look around, and her stomach sank when she saw Bill lying on the floor in a puddle of blood. And then, the sound of footsteps as they slowly drew near echoed in the silent room. With shallow breaths, Zaylie turned her head to see a pair of black work boots emerging from around the side of the kitchen island. She raised her eyes up, up, and up, until they met with Devon's cold stare.

"You killed him," she hissed. "You killed your own uncle."

His expression was dead as he looked down at her, as if life no longer existed inside. He was sweating profusely but seemed as calm as the ocean at low tide.

"You won't get away with this," she told him, her voice trembling. "They'll see you on the security cameras."

One side of Devon's mouth raised slightly as he said, "That's an easy fix. I'll erase the footage and tell them the real killer shot you and Uncle Bill and then got away before I could stop him. They'll believe me, Zaylie. I'm Bill's nephew, after all."

He'd barely gotten the last word out of his mouth when Smutti launched herself at the pantry door. Distracted by the sudden commotion, Devon spun around to face the pantry, giving Zaylie an opportunity to act. With adrenaline rushing through her veins, she jumped to her feet and shoved Devon backwards. He stumbled, and she took the few brief seconds offered her to turn and rush wildly from the room.

Her heart was pounding and her mind rushing so that she could barely make sense of where she was going or what she was doing. She leaped over Bill's body, but just as she paused long enough to try to grab his gun, Devon fired a shot and she felt the bullet whiz just past her ear. With a gasp, she left the gun and ran through the kitchen door.

He was coming after her; she could hear the pounding of his footsteps following closely behind. The front door was just ahead, but when she was only a few feet away, Devon fired another shot, shattering the glass window next to the door. Swiveling in another direction, Zaylie went the only other way she could, and that was up the stairs.

Just when Zaylie was barely past the third step, Devon grabbed her by the foot and yanked her downward. Her arms flailing as she stumbled, she snatched the nearby lamp off the table at the bottom of the stairs and cracked it over his head. He fell back with a moan, and Zaylie took her chance to run the rest of the way up the stairs.

The hall upstairs was dark and quiet, as if it had no idea of the danger that lurked below. Zaylie could hear Devon moaning as he gathered his senses, and she knew she didn't have much time. Within just a matter of seconds, his footsteps could be heard as he raced up the stairs after her.

Running to the end of the hallway, she quickly opened the door to the guest bedroom and stepped inside. She closed the door quietly behind her and hurried across the room where Rita had been staying. As she grabbed a large figurine from off the dresser and slipped into the closet, she could hear Devon opening each door along the hall.

Zaylie crouched down into the corner behind Rita's clothes and waited, her head spinning and chest tight. She clutched the figurine between both hands and closed her eyes for a moment as she fought against the panic that threatened to overtake her. It was so dark, and the tight quarters made it hard to breathe. For one breathtaking second, she was ten years old again and her sister's killer was closing in.

Rita's bedroom door squeaked, and Zaylie's eyes popped open. The overhead light clicked on inside the room, creating streaks through the slats in the closet door. She pressed her back against the wall, listening as his footsteps drew closer. Any second now, he would open the closet doors and find her. And then he would kill her.

She peered through the clothes and watched as his shadow came to stand before the closet doors. She readied herself to hit him with the figurine, but knew it wouldn't be enough. The lamp hadn't stopped him; she knew a little figurine wouldn't either. She had to try, though. She wouldn't go down without a fight.

"I know you're in there, Zaylie," he called out with a low laugh, and she felt her blood run cold.

She could see the shadow of his arm as it raised higher and higher, reaching out to push the folding door open. Suddenly, with no warning at all, the sound of a gunshot rang out, and she jerked back, watching in shock as his shadow slumped to the floor. And then, for an instant, everything was silent.

CHAPTER 34

Zaylie? Are you okay?"

At the sound of Bill's voice, Zaylie leaped to her feet and quickly opened the closet door. Devon lay on the floor with a bullet through his heart, and Zaylie stared at him for a moment, hardly able to believe it was all over. After twenty long years of not knowing what happened and searching for answers, Zoe's case could finally be put to rest. It seemed so surreal, and when Zaylie looked up at Bill, she could barely process her thoughts.

"Zaylie?" he asked again, and it was then she realized his head was bleeding.

"Uncle Bill," she whispered, stepping over Devon's body as she rushed to Bill's side. He wrapped her in his arms for a moment as they both cried, and then she pulled back to look up at him. "I'm okay," she said hoarsely as she reached up to touch the stream of blood on his temple. "Are *you*?"

Bill blew out a deep, shuddering breath, his eyes a bit glazed over as he looked across the room at Devon's dead body. "I killed him, Zaylie," he said, shaking his head. "My own nephew. I killed him."

With tears dripping down her cheeks, Zaylie took his hand and led him from the room. "You had no choice," she told him. "He shot you, Uncle Bill, and he was going to kill me. You did what you had to."

As they walked slowly down the stairs, both holding on to the other for support, Bill said in a bewildered tone, "I just can't believe it. After all these years of searching for the monster who killed your sister, it turns out it was my own flesh and blood."

They'd just reached the bottom of the stairs when the front door opened and Gran stepped inside. Her eyes were wide as she took in the shattered glass around the front door. When she looked up and spotted the blood on Bill's head and Zaylie's disheveled appearance, the color left her cheeks.

"What's happened?" she wanted to know as she rushed to their side.

"It's over, Gran," Zaylie said, tears filling her eyes once again as she gave her grandmother's hand a squeeze. "It's all over."

Two weeks later

Zaylie kneeled down and placed the bouquet of sunflowers on her sister's grave. Her mother and father were there, too, along with Gran and Bill, and the five of them were all filled with a variety of emotions. It was hard to believe it had been twenty years since they'd seen Zoe's beautiful smile and heard the tinkling sound of her laughter. She'd been taken from them at such a young age, just when she was on the brink of womanhood and doing amazing things with her life. If she'd lived, what would she be doing now? Would she be the artist she'd always hoped to be, or would her life have taken a different turn? Would she have married Clark and now be the mother of a handful of redheaded kids with overactive imaginations and a love for art? They would never know, but at least they could truly put her to rest now.

Zaylie caught a bit of movement out of the corner of her eye, and she turned to see Clark standing beneath a tree several yards away. He was Captain Jack, the man her sister had loved, and Zaylie knew he'd loved her, too, which was why he'd never married. Zaylie, her dad, and Bill had talked to him after Devon's death, and he'd thanked them for finally uncovering the truth.

"I think about her all the time," he'd told them, his eyes filled with sadness. *"I've always regretted not being there for her that night. If I'd known what Devon and Cameron had in mind, I'd have killed them both myself."*

Her mind turning to Cameron then, Zaylie thought about his interrogation with Bill two days after Devon's death. He'd let Zaylie listen in, and she could still see the expression of guilt on Cameron's face.

"I didn't realize what we were doing," he'd confessed. *"We were trying out a new drug, and we*

were both out of our heads. *After we grabbed Zoe, I took more of the drug and was passed out cold by the time we made it back to my house. I swear I had nothing to do with anything else that took place that night. When I came to the next day and heard that she was missing, Devon promised she was still alive and that they'd find her soon. After they found her body, I wanted to explain what happened, but Devon said they'd give him the death penalty. I couldn't do that to him, so I kept quiet.*" Tears were streaming down Cameron's cheeks at that point, and he buried his face in his hands. "*It's haunted me ever since, which is why I straightened myself out and have tried to pay penance for what we did.*"

"*How have you paid penance?*" Bill wanted to know.

"*I help abused women start a new life,*" he'd replied, wiping his eyes. "*I decided a long time ago that I wasn't doing anyone any favors by being a rich, selfish jerk, so I decided to spend my money by helping people.*"

After checking into Cameron's story, Bill confirmed that it was true. In the last eighteen years, Cameron had helped over three hundred women all over the world to escape their abusive circumstances. There were several cases that Bill refused to discuss, which let Zaylie know there had been children involved as well. After talking it over with her dad, who then discussed it with her mom, they all decided to forgive Cameron for his involvement in Zoe's kidnapping. If Zoe could have a say, Zaylie felt that she'd be happy her death held some meaning for others. Because of what happened to her, hundreds of lives had been changed for the better.

"Are you okay, honey?" Zaylie's dad asked as he slipped an arm around her shoulders.

Zaylie nodded. She knew he was referring not only to Zoe but also to the fact that her mom had agreed to come to their little graveside service. She hadn't tried to talk to Zaylie alone; she'd simply shown up that morning and had mostly remained silent since. Zaylie knew this was hard for her; it was hard for all of them. They'd all tried to move on with their lives, but this had continued to hang over their heads like a black cloud. They'd grown used to that cloud, and now finally being able to say goodbye was almost like saying goodbye to Zoe all over again.

Gran opened her Bible and read Revelation 21:4 and also John 11:25-26. Zaylie closed her eyes and allowed the tears to flow freely as she basked in the comfort of God's promise to some day wipe away all tears.

After Gran finished, they all said a prayer and turned to leave. Zaylie kissed her hand and pressed her fingers against Zoe's headstone, whispering goodbye to her sister one final time before following the others. Just before she got into her car, Zaylie looked back at the graveyard one more time and smiled, knowing she would see Zoe again.

CHAPTER 35

The following afternoon, Zaylie was getting ready to go to Erica's house to help pack up her belongings. After everything that had happened, Erica had decided to sell the house and move into an apartment, and Bill had asked for volunteers to help. Zaylie, her dad, Gran, and all the Steeles would be there, plus a few more helping hands.

Just as Zaylie was finishing tying up her hair, a soft knock sounded on her door.

"Just a minute," Zaylie called, her mouth half full of bobby pins.

She quickly finished pinning the rest of her hair in place and hurried to answer the door. As soon as she opened it, she blinked in surprise when she saw her mother standing on the other side.

"Mom," she stammered.

Tucking a strand of graying strawberry blonde hair behind one ear, Stephanie said, "I, uh, was about to leave, but I wanted to talk to you first. Do you have a minute?"

Zaylie nodded and stepped aside, allowing her mother to enter. Closing the door behind them, she turned to look at Stephanie, wondering what she wanted to say.

Stephanie wouldn't look at Zaylie as she slowly

walked around the room. After a moment, she cleared her throat and said, "A few years ago, you said it seemed like I blamed you for Zoe's death. Did you really feel that way?"

Zaylie crossed her arms protectively across her chest and said softly, "Yes."

Stephanie looked up at Zaylie then, and the pain in her eyes was haunting. "To keep from blaming myself, I think perhaps I did blame you a little," she whispered.

Zaylie's brow lowered. "Why would you blame yourself?" she asked.

Stephanie took a deep breath and blew it out slowly. "It was my idea for your dad and me to go into Savannah that night," she replied. "He didn't feel comfortable leaving the two of you out here alone, but I convinced him it would be alright."

Zaylie's heart squeezed in her chest, and she stepped forward, reaching out to touch her mom's arm. "It wasn't your fault, Mom," she said gently. "It was neither of our faults."

Tears filled Stephanie's eyes, and she roughly brushed them away. "I shouldn't have run away like I did, either," she stated in a hard tone, pulling her arm away from Zaylie. "I just couldn't stand the memories. Hopefully, you'll be able to forgive me some day."

With those words, Stephanie turned and left the room. Zaylie watched her go, wondering if she should say something, but her brain seemed unable to think of the right words. After a moment, she went over to her window and watched as her mom climbed into the back of an Uber before it drove away. It had been a long time since they'd spoken, and even longer since they'd really connected. Maybe now that the ice had been broken, so to speak, they could slowly start to rebuild their relationship.

An hour later, Zaylie, her dad, Gran, and Rita joined Bill and the others at Erica's house. There were several people there, including old Mr. Winters, Helen Buchanan, and a few other retirees. Zaylie noticed how Mr. Winters made certain to work close to Gran, and she couldn't help but smile at how cute it was.

"We just moved in, and now I'm already leaving," Erica stated with a sigh as she helped Zaylie fill a box with dishes in the kitchen.

"I'm sorry, Erica," Zaylie told her. "I know this has got to be hard for you."

"I just can't believe Devon…" Erica stopped and shook her head, and nothing else was said on the matter.

After the box was loaded, Zaylie said she needed to use the restroom.

"Use the one in my bedroom," Erica said. "Helen and Mr. Steele are packing up the hall bathroom."

Nodding, Zaylie walked from the kitchen and down the hall. When she stepped into the main bedroom, she noticed that nothing was packed up in this room yet. Everything was still as it had been, and when she spotted Devon's shoes resting in the corner, as if waiting for him to return, she shivered slightly.

Wishing to hurry, she walked quickly through the room toward the bathroom, gasping when her elbow struck Erica's jewelry box that sat on the dresser. She spun around and tried to catch it, but she wasn't quick enough. It clattered to the floor, spilling all its contents onto the rug.

With a moan, Zaylie dropped to her knees and quickly began cleaning up the mess. When she picked up the jewelry box to replace a ring and two bracelets, she noticed a small opening in the bottom of the box and realized it had a false bottom. Curiosity getting the better of her, she slid it open further until a tiny piece of jewelry slid out and bounced along the floor. Staring at the shiny little heart charm, Zaylie slowly leaned forward and picked it up. She flipped it over in her hand and gasped; engraved on the opposite side were the initials "C.S. + Z.L.".

Just then, the bedroom door opened and Zaylie looked up to find Erica standing in the doorway. She slowly took in the jewelry scattered on the floor, and then she saw the heart charm in Zaylie's hand. Her face immediately went pale, but she pretended as if all was well.

"Everything okay?" she asked nonchalantly.

Zaylie slowly stood to her feet and held the charm out for Erica to see. "Where did you get this?" she asked.

Erica glanced at the charm and shrugged. "I believe Zoe gave it to me," she replied.

Zaylie shook her head. "That's a lie, Erica," she stated firmly. "This charm was on Zoe's bracelet the night she was kidnapped. I saw it."

Erica slowly raised her cool blue eyes until they were trained on Zaylie's face. "I guess you just don't remember correctly, Zaylie," was her simple reply.

Zaylie closed her fist around the charm, clutching it tightly in her hand. "Were you there that night?" she rasped. "Did you know all along what happened?"

"No, I wasn't there," Erica quickly said. "You can ask my parents. I was home all evening."

Zaylie opened her mouth to respond, but then she stopped when it struck her like a blow to the chest. If Erica wasn't involved with the kidnapping, that meant she had to be involved with the *murder.*

"I took her out to the park, but she wasn't dead when I left her there. I swear, Zaylie."

Devon's words echoed through her mind, and Zaylie felt as if the world was collapsing all around her.

"Did *you* kill her, Erica?" she asked incredulously. "Did you somehow discover what happened, and you went to where Devon dumped the body and killed her?"

Erica glanced away, but not before Zaylie saw a look of panic flash through her eyes. She was trying to hold on to her composure, but Zaylie could feel her struggle. The tension in the room almost made the air sizzle, and Zaylie was about to push the subject further when Bill and her father suddenly entered the room.

"What's going on?" Bill immediately wanted to know when he saw their faces.

Holding the heart charm out for him to see, Zaylie said, "I found this in a hidden compartment in Erica's jewelry box. It's Zoe's. Bill, she was wearing it the night she was kidnapped." Looking at Erica, she said in a firm tone, "Tell him, Erica. Tell him that you're the one who really killed Zoe."

Bill's eyes widened with shock, and Zaylie's dad moved further into the room to stand by her.

"You're crazy," Erica snapped. "Why would I kill Zoe? She was my best friend."

"Because you thought Cameron gave her this charm, didn't you?" Zaylie shook her head as it all finally started to make sense. "You were in love with him, but he ignored you and kept trying to flirt with Zoe. When her mysterious boyfriend gave her this charm, you thought it was from Cameron. You wanted her out of the way so you could have a chance with him. Is he your son's father?"

Erica's jaw was clenched tightly, and she gave Zaylie a steely glare. "You can't prove any of this," she stated. "Maybe I should sue you for making such horribly false accusations. Now get out of my house."

Zaylie's dad placed his hand on her back and whispered, "Let's go, honey."

Zaylie looked up at him, feeling hurt by the expression in his eyes. He didn't believe her. He thought she still couldn't let it all go. Filled with frustration, Zaylie looked over at Bill and was surprised to find him studying Erica suspiciously.

"We have an unknown person's DNA from the crime scene," he said, and everyone stopped to stare at him. "It was found on Zoe's body but was never mentioned until now. Why don't we test it against yours, Erica? That way, you can prove all that you've just said."

Erica blinked and shifted uncomfortably. Zaylie knew Bill was bluffing; there was never any DNA found at the scene.

"No," Erica finally said through gritted teeth. "I don't have to do that."

"Evidence was found in your possession," Bill pressed. "If presented to a judge, he could force you to have those tests done."

Her face turning red with anger, Erica spun around to face Bill as she spat out, "You always hated me, didn't you? I was never good enough for your precious little nephew. Well, he may not have killed Zoe, but he left her out there to die and he murdered those other women. He was pathetic, and I despised him."

"How did you know where Zoe was?" Zaylie asked, her entire body trembling.

"Devon," Erica replied, rolling her eyes in

disgust. "He called me early the next morning, crying and begging me to go help her. When I got there, she was still alive, but barely."

Erica's expression darkened then, and Zaylie knew she was remembering that morning. The morning she killed her.

"I hated her, too," she hissed. "All the guys wanted her, but I never could figure out why. What did she have that I didn't? So, I took the pillow that I kept in my car and I finished the job. Then I took that stupid charm off her bracelet. Cameron loved me, you know. He told me so after Zoe was out of the picture. But he's just not the settling down type, so when I found out I was pregnant, I made Devon marry me. He never knew Kyle wasn't his son, not until recently."

Taking the handcuffs he always kept with him from his back pocket, Bill snapped them onto Erica's wrists and led her out to his car. With tears streaming down her cheeks, Zaylie leaned against her father's chest and sobbed. She could hear Rita running down the hall, wanting to know what was going on, but she couldn't talk to anyone. Not yet.

"I can't believe this," her dad said in a choked whisper against her hair. "All this time, it was the girl we thought was Zoe's best friend. How could she have done this?"

Zaylie shook her head but didn't answer. She was too shaken and heartbroken to make any sense of her words. The last two weeks had been a rollercoaster...no, the last twenty years had been.

Now that it was finally over, once and for all, she felt limp and lifeless. And totally blindsided.

Moments later, Zaylie's dad led her out to his car and drove her home. As they neared the house, Zaylie realized she still held the heart charm in her hand. Looking down, she opened her palm and gently touched the charm with her forefinger as another tear dripped slowly from her cheek.

The truth will set you free, she thought, and with a deep, shuddering breath, she looked out the window and spotted a small patch of sunflowers in a field they were driving by. She'd never noticed them before, but their bold, beautiful colors instantly made her think of her sister, and she couldn't help but smile.

EPILOGUE

Fall was just around the corner, and that slight break in the weather caused a sense of excitement to stir through Zaylie's body. She loved it when the air started to get cooler and all things pumpkin began breaking into the scene. The church would be hosting a fall picnic in a few weeks, with hayrides, bonfires, and games. She could hardly wait; this would be the first time she'd attended in several years.

It was official. She was staying on Whisper Island and opening a second training center. Gran was over the moon, and Zaylie could hardly wait to get started. They would have to build it all first, which would take several months, but the permits were all in place and they were breaking ground today.

"This is so exciting!" Rita squealed as she, Zaylie, and Gran watched from afar. She'd moved into her own place last month, but she still came by several times a week. Zaylie was thrilled to have her best friend living on the island, as well, even if she did happen to have an annoying twin brother.

The work crew began digging, and the three women went to sit on the back deck of the house to watch. The breeze from the river blew gently across their skin as they sipped on sweet tea and lemonade and talked about Rita's new job at the school. Sand gnats and mosquitos buzzed around, but Zaylie had installed a patio repellent which kept the pesky bugs at bay. The women were so engrossed in their conversation that they didn't notice the sounds of the digging equipment had suddenly died down.

"Mrs. Ferguson? Miss Layne?" the supervisor called, and they turned to look at him. "Y'all might want to take a look at this."

Wondering what was going on, the three women hurried over to the work site to find the men all gathered around something. They stepped aside when the women joined them and looked down into the freshly dug ground.

"Oh, my Lord, what is that?" Rita gasped, covering her mouth.

Half-buried among the freshly uprooted grass and dirt was what appeared to be the skeletal remains of a human body.

"Gran," Zaylie said, her eyes wide, "I may be wrong, but I believe we just found Great Aunt Azalea."

A NOTE FROM THE AUTHOR

Thank you so much for reading "Killer Trail". If you enjoyed it, please leave a review on Amazon or Goodreads – or both! Reviews really help! I look forward to hearing from you. If you're interested in receiving news of upcoming books, discounts, free e-books and more, please sign up for my newsletter at:

https://newsletter.jennyelaineauthor.com/

Made in the USA
Monee, IL
05 November 2024